LEGITIMATE
Bush Woman

LEGITIMATE
Bush Woman

The lighter side
of life on the land

RAELENE HALL

First published 2007 by
KMK Publishing
Ned's Creek Station, Meekatharra WA 6642
nedscreekstn@bigpond.com
www.outbackwriter.com

Edited and designed by Janet Blagg
Cover art and design by Gail Breese
Illustrations by Maureen Woods
Produced by Yellow Wallpaper Editing and Publishing
Printed by Griffin Press

National Library of Australia
Cataloguing-in-publication data

> Hall, Raelene.
> Legitimate bush woman : the lighter side of life on the land.
>
> 1st ed.
> ISBN 9780646477985 (pbk.).
>
> 1. Hall, Raelene. 2. Rural women - Western Australia -
> Meekatharra Region - Anecdotes. 3. Ranches - Western
> Australia - Meekatharra Region - Anecdotes. I. Woods,
> Maureen (Maureen Mary), 1944- . II. Title.
>
> 920.72

All the pieces in this book first appeared as a monthly column entitled 'Station Life' in the Geraldton *Midwest Times* between 2002 and 2007.

The publication of this book was assisted by a grant from the Connellan Airways Trust (www.connellanairwaystrust.org.au) which sponsors and supports the activities of people living in remote areas of Australia.

Part of the proceeds of the sale of this book donated to the Royal Flying Doctor Service (Western Operations).

This book is dedicated to the
memory of my sister Irene
and my brother Phil

Raelene Hall lives in outback Western Australia. She has written articles for print and online publications in Australia and overseas on education, outback life, communications, nature, spirituality, families, technology and the environment. She was a columnist for a regional newspaper for five years and currently edits and publishes *Pedals*, the magazine of the Isolated Children's Parents' Association.

Contents

Foreword

I am thrilled to write a Foreword to *Legitimate Bush Woman*. I have known of Raelene's intention to make this book for some time now, but like many other things in life, it wasn't happening as quickly as anticipated, due to the many things that a bush woman has on her agenda. A couple of family tragedies gave Raelene the jolt necessary to take stock and do what must be done. I'm glad she did.

I never cease to admire the bush women of Australia. The most impressive thing about them is that they do not feel they are very special. They just lead comprehensive, admirable lives, based on a pioneering tradition that says you look for the good in others rather than the bad. They have a laugh if possible, even in the tightest of situations. They learn to cope in every type of emergency. They share a camaraderie with other women no less than that of the Anzacs. They value family above all else. That keeps most of them so busy that they don't have time to assess their own performances and wouldn't want to anyway. That might take them into skiting and they've got too much common sense for that sort of nonsense.

All of those qualities emerge in Raelene's writing. The whimsical, the poignant, the straight-up funny bits are all presented with an accuracy that can only come with the broad experience. These are great stories and they are an illustrator's dream. My only complaint is that there are not enough stories, so readers out there — please buy up all the copies of this book and let Raelene get on with the next volume.

Cheers!
Ted Egan AO
Administrator of the Northern Territory

Acknowledgements

I've been planning this book in my mind for a few years but circumstances and procrastination (at which I am an expert) have put it on hold numerous times, but in 2007 it became a reality. To the wonderful people who have supported me in so many ways over the years this one is for you.

To my legitimate bush husband and kids who are always there for me.

To Maureen for her terrific drawings and the great laughs we enjoy together.

To Janet for being a wonderful editor and mentor.

To Gail for my marvellous cover and logo.

To Dianne and Alan for inspiring the title.

To Ted, Rachael and Merelyn for your contributions and support.

To Marg McAllister, writing tutor, mentor and friend.

To all my writing friends, wherever you may be, thank you for your love, friendship and support over many years.

To Lara and her wonderful team at the *Midwest Times* — without you none of this would have taken place.

Introduction
I Feel a Column Coming On

I've always been a writer — of sorts. I recall writing compositions (that's what they were called back then) at school that went on for pages and pages. My motto was 'Length Equals Quality' and so I always had to write more than anyone else in my class. I don't recall what sort of response these elicited from my teachers — probably huge sighs at the thought of having to plough all the way through them in order to mark them!

A few years ago I had cause to visit Kalgoorlie, which just happened to be the home of one of my primary school headmasters. He had, for some bizarre reason known only to himself, actually kept one of my composition books, and took great pleasure (perhaps almost a masochistic pleasure) in taking it out of the cupboard and reading me an excerpt from one of my stories. In this particular story I'd written that when I grew up I wanted to be an animal trainer! As I was working with children at the time I wondered if perhaps I was part way to that ambition!

In my student years I wrote poetry — very bad poetry I might add — with titles like 'The Golden Days',

'Forsaken Love', What is Love?', 'Lingering Memories', 'First Love' and 'The Heartbreaker'. I'm not sure who the last-named was based on, except that it was a female — it certainly wasn't me.

After school my writing mainly consisted of letters to family and friends, most notable for the fact that I answered letters the minute I received them. Friends cursed me for making them feel as though they should do the same — not that many of them did. But justice was served, as it usually is if you wait long enough, for now I know just how they felt when someone expects an answer to an email right away! I just think, 'Oh, go away for a few days!'

As well as a writer of sorts I was of course a reader and I read anything I could get my hands on including penny dreadful romances where woman meets man, woman loathes man, woman falls in love with man against her better judgement, man is too thick/stubborn to realise it but eventually man and woman both recognise they are in love and live happily ever after. Many of these books had the romantic outback of Australia as their setting.

So when city life didn't agree with me and the opportunity arose to work in this great romantic setting I jumped at it. For several years I worked on outback properties and although life wasn't quite the way it was portrayed in those romance books I had a lot of fun and adventures and I did meet my 'outback' man. Whilst not exactly tall, dark and handsome, he certainly made my heart beat faster and my romantic soul decided life with him on his outback cattle station was for me. It's probably just as well I had my rose coloured glasses on or I'd have run a million miles. Mind you, there are probably times he wishes I'd run too!

So I settled into married life on the property, all set to become a truly legitimate bush woman. I cleaned my new house religiously, planted a garden (most of it died), pored over the CWA cookbook to turn out traditional sponges, lamingtons, scones and other goodies (most of which were total disasters). I tried to learn about station life and how to do it, only to discover that whatever key part of the brain you needed to be a real bush woman — it was missing from mine.

I couldn't find my way more than a stone's throw from home. I was terrified if they took me out mustering. Despite endless instructions I couldn't tell the sex of a cow (!) unless it or I was upside down — and wonder now why the hell I needed to know it anyway. And I nearly died every time summer came around. Ha! The romantic outback, I decided, was best viewed from the homestead with green lawns, a bough shed for summer and a kero heater and wood stove for winter.

The arrival of children, I thought, would tie me to the house. Well, it did — but only if I wanted to be there on my own, because the children were soon out and about on the station, learning all the things their mother never could.

It was around then, with my ego battered and bruised, I decided it was time to get back into something I enjoyed and found satisfying, something I felt I had a modicum of talent for. And so I did a number of writing courses over the years, always enjoying them but not quite knowing what to do when they finished. It never occurred to me that while doing courses was obviously beneficial, you actually had to practise writing like everything else.

In 2000 I did a course on writing for children. Well, how hard could that be? Look at picture books: a few words and a few pictures — nothing to it. It was a very rude awakening to find that writing for children was every bit as hard as writing for adults and picture books were in a difficulty category all of their own. Still, I persevered and I graduated from the course, very clear that writing for children really wasn't for me.

Which left the awkward question — what did I want to write about/for? Another course with the tutor from Children's Writing allowed me to explore that exact question and it wasn't long before I discovered that what I *liked* writing was non-fiction articles and humour. Gradually I started to enjoy some success in this field and see some of my work published.

A couple of years later I boldly (it's quite easy to be bold via email!) contacted some magazines and newspapers with my work. I was looking for a regular writing spot and fortune smiled on me in the form of Lara Brncic, editor of the *Midwest Times* in Geraldton, who was brave enough to give a newcomer a monthly column in the paper. My column was to be a light-hearted look at life on the land from my 'legitimate bush woman' point of view.

Five years later, encouraged by the feedback I've received from many people over the years about how they have enjoyed the column, I have taken 'leave of absence' in order to put this book together. You can blame it on a friend of mine who asked me when I was going to put the columns into a book — which was rather a light bulb moment for me. I'm not sure if she was serious but guess who is going to be the first to be visited with the guilties if she doesn't buy several copies!

I also blame those who told me they enjoyed the columns: this is your punishment! I couldn't believe it when I got fan mail — well, a couple of letters and emails constitutes fan mail in my eyes — and have safely tucked them away for posterity. One which still makes me smile referred to how they enjoyed reading my column as a change from all the usual cr— they were required to read, like office paperwork. Now that's what I call a compliment.

On the odd visit to Geraldton my name occasionally rang a bell with someone when we were introduced, but the biggest shock came when someone said they recognised me — from my photo that came with my column in the paper! The photo wasn't one of my better ones (mind you, they don't get a lot better) so it was a bit of a dubious thrill to be recognised from it. Still, I guess we all have to start somewhere, and even Hollywood starlets get recognised from their less gorgeous photos at times!

People have asked me how I came up with the ideas each month, and I have to tell them truthfully that it really wasn't that hard because they kind of wrote themselves. I could never tell you in advance what a particular column was going to be about. (Quite often I thought it

5

was going to be a blank page because my ideas bank was running on dry.) Somehow, though, before the deadline (milliseconds before, at times), there was always something that made me think, 'Aha, I feel a column coming on.' Friends and family got to know that look and would start protesting right away. 'Don't you *dare* put that in your column!'

Once the trigger clicks it's full steam ahead wherever I happen to be. Columns have been written on scraps of paper in the car (I wasn't driving), at school camps, in hotels and on planes, in the garden and the kitchen and of course in the office, where the computer is.

For those readers who have enjoyed my columns I hope you enjoy this book just as much. I know you will get a laugh from the wonderful illustrations by my good friend Maureen Woods. For those who haven't read any of my columns, I hope you get as much pleasure from the pieces in this book as I have from putting them all together.

An Aussie Tradition

In a recent newsletter, the rector of our son's school queried why men found it necessary to kick the tyres of all the machinery they looked at. (He had just paid a visit to the Dowerin Machinery Field Day.) Being Irish — and he thinks we have some strange habits! — he wouldn't understand that it is an Australian tradition and there doesn't need to be a reason for it. It's just one of those things you do. I actually think it might be a true blue male initiation type of act.

'Now look here son, before you can be called a real man, you've got to learn to kick tyres. You do it this way and always with your boots on. It isn't cool to kick a tyre then hop around holding on to your foot.'

It's a man's way of letting everyone know that while this machinery may look large they are still the boss.

I'm not a male but I also kick tyres. Why? For two reasons: one, because it makes me look like I know what I'm doing, so at least I look like a true Aussie bush woman, and two, it might just give me a clue as to whether the tyre I'm kicking is about to go flat. If it is about to go flat then I can try to make sure there's a male handy to change it for me — I got left out in the cold when women's lib came in.

Those in the know (my husband and sons) tell me you can always tell when a tyre is starting to go flat. Well of course you can, because it makes that horrible clunk, clunk sound and suddenly the car won't go where you want it to go. However I'm told that I 'should' be able to tell a tyre is going flat long before this stage, and not have to wait until the rim is digging holes in the road and I've left a trail of rubber for the past three kilometres.

I don't know why manufacturers can't put a warning signal in the car for flat tyres like they do everything else. I get beeped if I leave the lights on, flashed if I don't fasten my seat belt and am pursued by flashing lights and wailing sirens if I speed — a very cunning element of the car set up!

Surely it can't be that difficult to install some little gadget in each tyre which is connected to the dashboard, programmed with a gentle and reassuring voice. 'Excuse me, but your left hand front tyre is going to go flat in five minutes. Slow down now and pull over and change the tyre and all will be well.' If I find out that anyone releases such a thing on the market in the next little while, be warned I'll be in line for my share of the royalties for copyright of such a brilliant idea.

Meanwhile I'll go on kicking tyres just to prove what a true blue Aussie woman I am.

I Hereby Resolve

New Year comes around and that eternal question arises yet again. 'What's your New Year resolution?' Well this year I have seen the light (finally) and I have made only one resolution: 'Not to make any New Year's Resolutions!' It's the simplest solution and the best — because if you don't make them you can't break them. Every year I make all these wonderful resolutions and what happens? They last an hour, a day or, most rarely, a week.

The first one of course is always about dieting. I'm going to lose weight — *after* New Year, when we've finished the Christmas left overs, once I've polished off the kid's lollies from Santa (don't want them rotting their teeth) or before I have another birthday.

Then there is the exercise resolution, whereby I will go for a brisk walk every day. Every day, that is, if my feet aren't hurting, it isn't too hot or cold, I don't have an urgent deadline to meet or when I can get myself out of bed early enough.

What about the promise to the family that I will cook more cakes/biscuits? Hmm, that one isn't even a candidate for the starting gate when it's 45 degrees outside and even hotter in my kitchen and they would get eaten before I could even get the last one out of the oven. I think I must have had heat stroke to have even let that thought cross my mind. Much more sensible if I just order biscuits on the mail truck.

That reminds me of another resolution I always make and which never lasts (in fact it too doesn't usually get past the start). I will do my mail and have it ready more than five minutes before it is due to be collected. That might have a chance if only I could catch up with all the Christmas mail I didn't get written and send off cards to those people inconsiderate enough to have birthdays just after Christmas and New Year.

Perhaps I shouldn't be so quick to knock resolutions though. Maybe my kids have made a resolution to keep their rooms tidy, or to do the dishes on a daily basis, or not squabble with each other all day, every day — it would be a terrible shame to discourage them if they were really keen!

Or my husband might be planning resolutions like air conditioning our entire house, taking over the teaching in the schoolroom or maybe booking us both on a long romantic cruise to the South Seas.

Now I know I have definitely been out in the sun too long!

Computer Overload

I have to confess to being just a bit of a computer junkie — I can't imagine my life these days without one. However things are getting out of hand around here at present — they are breeding — the computers I mean!

So far I have my own desktop computer, a laptop, my daughter's old school computer and now her brand new, bells and whistles model. Then there's the laptop my son has at boarding school and the new one I'm getting next month.

My desktop computer has been playing up for months. I think it is just temperamental and feels overworked and under serviced so as payback it shuts down whenever it feels like it, and starts up only when it is good and ready. Of course it shuts down right in the middle of something important (like my column which was due yesterday) and have I saved my work? — of course I have — not!

It's been to the computer doctor at least twice and had its motherboard replaced (I'm told the mother board is the thing that makes everything work — well naturally!) but it still isn't happy. It hasn't got a virus and I keep its vaccinations up to date so I'm not sure what more it expects of me. Maybe the fatherboard has upset the motherboard?

I've taken off its casing and peered at its innards like I know what I'm doing, rattled a few bits and pieces, blew some (well a lot of) dust out and replaced its covers, which cured the ills for a day or so but now it is up to the same old trick.

The computer doctor is a bit too far away for me to just 'drop' it into the surgery for a check-up and I dare not phone any computer guru for instructions over the phone. That's one way to guarantee it will never work again!

However I've learnt to beat it at its own game. If you think computers are just electronic gadgets then tell me how you explain this: my computer has a hissy fit and won't start. 'Okay,' I say, 'that's fine.' Then I just casually saunter next door into the schoolroom, all the while talking quietly to myself. 'Well that heap of old junk doesn't want to work, who cares? I can always use this one. It's bigger, better, faster and cleaner.' After spending half an hour oohing and aahing over the wonders of the new computer I meander back into my office, still muttering to myself, 'Suppose I'd better give this old heap of junk another try before I chuck it out the door.'

One flick of the switch and my computer is running like Herb Elliott. I could almost swear there was a certain sheepish look about my desktop — wonder why that would be?

Annie Get Your Gun

I've decided life is too short not to try new activities, so when a friend recently asked me if I wanted to try my hand at pistol shooting, I quickly said yes before my brain could veto the idea. When my friend had recovered from the shock — I'm sure she only asked because she expected a resounding 'No' — she showed me the basics.

I carefully took in all the advice she gave me and watched as she and other members of her club set up their equipment. I must admit to some concern when I saw they had all set up what looked like mini telescopes on little tables about waist high, and I was busy trying to figure out how you looked through those and fired a gun at the same time!

It was a relief to see that you didn't actually use the two items at the same time — the telescope was to see how accurate your aim at the target had been. I thought perhaps a long range telescope might be useful to see what I'd hit.

After showing me how to load the pistol, how to put the safety catch on, and how to stand and aim, I was ready. Standing sideways, hand on hip, gun raised, I fired — where to no one knows, but fortunately there were no birds flying by as they may have been unlucky enough to collide with a stray bullet.

At my second attempt things improved and holes actually appeared in the target. I was assured they were put there by me and that my target hadn't been shared with someone else. 'This isn't so hard,' I thought as I lined up again and promptly missed the target with every shot.

Feeling incredibly proud of myself nonetheless I was bragging of my Annie Oakley-like prowess to hubby when I returned home.

'What sort of pistol was it?' he asked. Men ask the dumbest questions sometimes.

'One that fires bullets,' I replied. I don't know why he had that look on his face. After all, if I asked him the colour of the dress I'd worn to the last party we went to bet he couldn't tell me — and that is surely of more consequence than the type of pistol I was using!

Beating the Bathers Blues

The ultimate summer test has arrived. Do my bathers still fit? It's a shock to reveal the post-winter body and bathers have a habit of showing every lump, bump and roll of your body's landscape. In fact not only are these fault lines visible, they seem to expand in magnitude the minute you step into bathers.

Shopping for bathers is something I prefer not to put myself through more often than I have to, which is why I tend to wear them until they resemble something my mother would have dusted with before I begin the search for a new pair.

As summer warms up, out come the ads insisting, 'We have bathers to suit every body type,' then proceeding to show you six assorted styles ranging from the Claytons bikini to the bikini that actually uses a scrap of fabric to a one-piece that may have actually used two complete handkerchiefs. All are modelled by the same perfectly formed, sculpted, toned gorgeous bodies. I may be blonde, I may be female, I may not always be the brightest match in the box — but even I know they aren't going to look that good on me. If they did I wouldn't be writing columns, I'd be prancing on the cat walk!

So it's off to the stores, skulking around the racks

searching for the ultimate bathers. You know, the ones that make you look as if you have just lost a stone in a minute. If you manage to find something halfway reasonable you then have to actually get into them, an act requiring the flexibility of a Houdini. You look in the mirror under lights designed to draw out your every blemish, only to realise they don't hide any figure challenges, they just relocate them. Your boobs are now under your armpits and your tummy rolls are where your boobs should be. Some women don't seem to care but I like to know all my 'bits' are where Mother Nature intended them to be or somewhere in that vicinity anyway.

After hours of misery I finally find a pair I think would not be responsible for scaring anyone too much if they were to see me in them. On stepping out of the change room I see a sleek young thing in the exact same pair of bathers, only hers are 4 sizes smaller and she looks like a million bucks in them.

'Aren't they lovely?' I smile at her. 'I just bought the same pair,' and grin evilly at the look of horror on her face as she looks me up and down, obviously picturing my body in them. Bet she doesn't buy them!

Sometimes you just have to find your own justice in this world!

Anyone Got an Oil Can?

I used to play hockey and netball once — or, as my kids so kindly put it, 'back in the olden days!'

Yesterday my daughter wanted to kick the soccer ball around between bouts of school work and so she dragged me out to be her soccer companion. We happily kicked the ball about for a while (five minutes seems like a while when you're not especially fit) before I decided it would be easier to throw and catch than to run after a ball.

Old habits die hard so I started passing the ball in my best netball fashion — crouching to catch the low ones and stretching for the high ones, returning them with lightning reflexes. I was getting into the swing of things but then we really had to stop. School work was calling, as was the water bottle and the loo. I felt terrific — I'd exercised and got my daughter exercising as well — it had been an all-round great mother/daughter bonding time.

At least it was until I woke up this morning and discovered I'd either been run over by a truck or every bone and joint had gone rusty. I creaked as I crawled out of bed and staggered to the bathroom. I sat gingerly on chairs, levered myself up like a ninety year old and suffered loudly — not that anyone was listening, not even the dog, who just went on sleeping in the sun when I tried to tell him my woes and why I couldn't bend down to pat him.

To add insult to injury I was going away the next day and had to wash the car which, due to its excess of height and my lack of it, involves climbing up and down a ladder — the muscles screamed louder than the music I had cranked up.

Old habits may die hard but some old habits should just — DIE!

Decisions Decisions

'Undies! You've got to write about undies,' a friend said after trying to buy some and finding there was no such thing as a basic pair of underpants any more. 'Once I used to just go in and grab one of those multi-packs and I was out of there. Not any more, now it's hipsters or briefs, prints or plain, cotton or silk, high rise or low rise.' She shook her head in sorrow; I thought perhaps I'd better not ask what she did end up with.

I know where she's coming from. You can't buy anything these days without having to make endless decisions. Take bread for instance — go to a baker and try asking for a loaf of bread.

'White, wholemeal or grain?'

'Ahh, umm, er, wholemeal.'

'Sliced or unsliced?'

'Um, sliced will do.'

'Poppy seeds, sesame seeds or no seeds?'

'I don't want to grow the darned stuff, just eat it.'

By this stage I've eaten the entire tray of tasters they leave on the counter.

Milk is another classic. First do you want white or coloured — green, pink or chocolate? Bottle or carton and what size? Now do you want hi-low or low-hi?

Calcium by the bucket load or the teaspoonful? Do you want it to build up your bones or protect your heart? I'm beginning to wonder if cows have anything to do with milk these days. While we're talking dairy products let's head to the cheese section. A good half hour disappears as I compare low fat, high fat, processed and non-processed, single slices , bulk, grated or block. By the time I'm finished I'm so fed up I throw whatever I've got in my hand into the trolley and bolt from the aisle, stressed and traumatised.

Remember when shampoo came in oily, normal and dry? Forget that. Now we have to decide whether we want moisture therapy, super shine, colour lock, anti-frizz, anti-flat, scalp care. I know what I want. I want to scream!

Walking past disposable nappies I heave a sigh of relief that I no longer need to buy them. I watch mothers, with whining child in the trolley, staring at the packages with a glazed expression on their faces. I'm sure they are thinking, 'I just want some damned nappies and I don't care if they have elastic legs, if they go pink or blue when they're wet or if they have some pretty picture on them.' Let's face it, the same product ends up in them regardless.

No wonder we are such a stressed lot. To me though, the last straw was the introduction of dual flush loos. The one place in your day where you can go and relax without having to make a single decision — your body did it all for you — and now you have to work out, half flush or full flush? Give us a break.

Time Thief

I once read a magazine in which Colette Mann the actress (hate these multi-talented people) wrote a column. She spent the whole column saying she had nothing to write about. I thought that was a good lurk so I sent in a similar column. My editor wasn't quite as keen on the idea. She just said, 'Write me a proper column.' No sense of fun, that lady.

That's okay though because I've got two whole days before my deadline — plenty of time. Only one problem though — I've been visited by the 'time thief'. Now you may laugh but I can prove he/she/it exists and I'm not the only one being picked on.

For example our mail truck arrives here early Thursday morning, which means having my mail ready Wednesday night (it's that or getting up at daybreak — no choice really). So how is it that every week when Wednesday rolls around I'm sitting up until all hours doing my mail? It's because the time thief snuck up and stole a couple of days out of my week. There are meant to be seven days in the week (or so they told me at school) but I'm sure there are only five between one mail day and the next and sometimes not even five.

The same thing happens with the months. At least

two or three months vanish every year. No sooner is Christmas over than stores are trying to prepare us for the next one. What happened to recovery time for humans and budgets? Then into the less-than-full new year the powers that be are trying to shove in a few more events to help out because now we have to have a day to celebrate everything. Only one they haven't come up with yet is Contemplating your Navel Day but give them time. Give us *all* time.

Of course if the time thief can steal hours, days and months then the next step up is pinching years. How else can I have adult children when I haven't got that much older, couldn't possibly have got old enough for adult children. Good heavens that would make me … oh, well never mind.

So there you have it. We aren't getting older, the world isn't spinning faster, and life isn't any more hectic. It's all down to that darned time thief.

When I get hold of it I'm going to demand all my missing time be returned to me. Just imagine, with all that extra time I'll not only catch up, I could even be ahead of myself. I could have next month's column done and dusted well before the deadline. Then I could be very generous and sell off any extra time I got back to those who are still struggling to get everything done. Maybe I could be known as the Time Bunny or the Time Fairy.

Car Shopping

It's that time of year again.

Time, that is, to put number two son back into boarding school, put daughter into day school and head out to do some serious damage to the bank account. This time it will not just be serious damage, it will be more like catastrophic — because we are about to buy a new car.

After seventeen years of faithful service the old white Hilux is getting retired. In fact it is very tired, and we're hoping it will be tired enough to keep number two son from getting into trouble when he gets his licence.

For some months therefore we have had numerous round-the-table discussions about what to buy — 2WD or 4WD, diesel/petrol, Holden/Toyota — progressing on to discussion in foreign language that the boys and hubby like to indulge in, with words like torque, tare and revolutions, wheel size and engine size.

Personally I can't see what all the fuss is about. It's fairly simple, in my book, what's required of a new car. It must be comfortable to sit in and look good when you're driving it. Air conditioning and heating are obviously not negotiable, as is a good sound system. It should have a convenient place for sunglasses, lipstick and mobile phone and a mirror in a suitable spot for redoing make-up.

The instrument panel should be straightforward — easy to understand at a glance — red light for a problem, green light for no problem is as complicated as it needs to get. A locking system that makes it impossible to lock your keys in the car would be helpful and an interior décor that won't clash with your outfits. Door handles designed so as not to break fingernails of course.

So while hubby and sons debate technicalities with the salesman I'll have made my decision. Who said women don't know how to buy cars? After all it's just shopping — right girls?

Mice Mayhem

We had a mouse hunt today. I stood outside the front door and yelled instructions while hubby and son tried, and failed, to catch it. So the mouse is still running loose but its days are numbered. I don't appreciate having to clean out my entire pantry because of these little grey beasts. I don't find their little black pebbles an attractive addition to the food shelves. Once in my house they are in enemy territory and it's war — them against me!

One has already gone to mouse heaven. He died in our bathroom — not sure what from but possibly from seeing the state of my bathroom floor, or perhaps he saw me in the shower (that would do it for sure), but either way he's gone. Trouble is he chose the bathmat as his final resting place and a family member, who shall remain nameless, didn't see him lying there. It wasn't me thank goodness but I did have the dubious honour of washing the bath mat that received his flattened corpse.

There's another mouse pushing her luck (they can't all be boy-mice, can they?); not only does she hide under the lounge, ready to give me heart failure by skittering by me as I sit down but even has the cheek to turn her nose up at the cheese on the trap. Admittedly it's only Home Brand but if it's good enough for us you'd darned well think it was good enough for a mouse.

First she pinched the cheese without setting the trap off, then removed the cheese and left it lying on the floor next to the trap — now that's really insulting. Even my kids aren't allowed to get away with that sort of table manners.

So a change of menu is required. Some people swear by pumpkin seeds or peanut butter. If it was a Yankee mouse you could try peanut butter and jelly (jam to us). If it was a true Aussie mouse it would prefer vegemite. Or maybe it would go for powdered milk, coconut, plain flour or sugar — after all, it's already sampled all these in the pantry.

Hopefully we can find something that appeals to her taste buds and will entice her to get stuck into the mousetrap smorgasbord. I do feel a little sorry for her, but she should know there is a law against home invasions and that home owners can use 'reasonable force' to protect themselves from invaders.

But once that 'reasonable force' has been carried out I do hope there is someone on hand to remove the deceased offender to an outdoor resting place. It doesn't have to the long arm of the law, just as long as it is a long arm and it isn't mine!

Where's the Savings?

Finally daylight saving is coming to an end. It has been touted as such a wonderful thing in our lives that I've been looking everywhere for the daylight I am meant to have saved over the past three months but I can't find it anywhere. I can find all the glass jars I save (which never get re-used) and the coins I save, even the Christmas cards I saved to recycle one day — but no daylight.

In fact daylight saving doesn't seem to have saved me anything at all which, all things considered, is a bit lousy. I thought it meant that for every minute of daylight I saved each day I could hoard it away and hey presto! Come a week when my schedule is really, really full and I'm pushing a loaded barrow uphill to get everything done and my column deadline is biting at my ear then I could just whip out an hour or two from my daylight saving bank and I'd be able to give myself some breathing space.

And if we are saving it shouldn't we be getting interest on it? The government should say, 'Well, you've saved ten hours so here's an extra week off for you!' I think that would be a sure-fire vote winner. Mind you, if it's anything like the interest you get on most other savings, it's so small you wouldn't notice it anyway or —

more likely — it wouldn't even cover all the extra fees or charges they slug you with these days. Now that's what I call daylight robbery!

I'm also puzzled about where we should put the daylight we've saved. It shouldn't really need refrigeration unless you want it to cash it in as a winter's day in the middle of summer — which, come to think of it, isn't a bad idea. Do you put it in the cupboard, under your bed or should it be stored 'this side up' in the shed?

Is it like a Fly Buy's scheme where if you don't spend it you lose it? Sorry you've held on to your daylight savings for too long so you've just lost it all. Never mind, come next year you can start all over again, and then there will be even more bonus ways to save your daylight, like not going to bed at all or moving to the Antarctic for six months of the year.

Perhaps by the time I retire I'll have enough daylight savings to live off in my old age — maybe I could sell it back to the government as part of my retirement fund!

Circle Work

'Circle work' is what they call it when young hot-blooded males with too much testosterone drive around in circles in vehicles with too many accessories and stickers. I'm not sure what's to be gained by it, but it's a skill most young Aussie men have practised at some stage of their life.

I decided if it was good enough for the young fellows then it was good enough for me, so I've taken up circle work myself. And found I am extremely good at it, in fact I'm so good I can even do it without the need of a vehicle.

I just walk around in ever decreasing circles until I meet up with myself, at which point I turn around and start going the other way. This is how I avoid all those jobs screaming to be completed (let alone started). If I know there is work awaiting me in the office I'll detour to the clothesline. When I see the washing waiting to be brought in and folded I find an urgent reason to be in the kitchen. If I get the feeling I should actually be doing something worthwhile in the kitchen, like cooking, I pick up some paperwork and take it to the office. See! Circle complete!

The biggest problem with my circle work is that I never achieve anything except a headache from getting too dizzy. That doesn't seem to be a worry for those who do it in vehicles, although they often seem to cop a delayed form of headache the morning after their circle work.

Actually, circle work has stopped being fun for me and is starting to get frustrating. With twenty-four hours left to pack and prepare for a week away it might really be good to actually go in a straight line for five minutes and achieve something.

The trip is not unexpected. I've known about it for months and I fully intended to stop circling some weeks ago and start getting a little organised by dragging out the iron, the suitcase, the ton of paperwork I needed to sort through and some clothes.

I think perhaps circle work could become one of those mental disorders where people are compelled to do the same thing over and over again without achieving anything constructive. (A good example are those people who insist on supporting footy teams who never get off the bottom rung of the ladder.)

So for a change I'd like to stop circling and be one of those people who progress in a straight line from A to B to C to D. Logical, straightforward people who arrive at their destination looking cool and calm, their luggage neatly packed and their paperwork in order. They always have a biro, never lose their sunglasses and you'll never find them rummaging in their bag for anything.

One day I'll figure out how they manage it (perhaps someone will hand me some government funding to research it), but in the meanwhile, if you see someone tearing into a room five minutes late, hair awry, shirt hanging out, digging through her bag, be sure to say 'Hi!' Fair chance it will be me.

Coffee Anyone?

I recently won a you beaut, super duper coffee maker. Not bad considering I didn't even know I'd entered the competition and I don't drink coffee. It was for subscribing to a magazine that I'd decided I didn't really like anyway. The subscription prize in the next issue was for a fantastic holiday — of course Murphy's Law dictates I wouldn't win that.

Don't get me wrong — I was very excited to win something and the minute it arrived I had it unpacked, plugged in and was trying to figure out how to use it. Logical son number two read the instructions while I fiddled. Between us we got it working, put in the coffee 'pods' (yep, sounds just like something you'd pick off a tree) and made coffee in the yuppie cups that came with it. It smelled wonderful and we both felt very clever, then we poured it down the sink.

After many years of nagging to cut down his coffee consumption, hubby is now asked every five minutes 'Would you like a cup of coffee?' I've even shown him how to use it — very generous of me, I think, to allow someone else to play with my new toy.

Yesterday there was no one home to make coffee for. No hubby, no visitors. I didn't think the dog would like coffee, although he does like tea so you never know. I decided to take the plunge (ha ha! get it!) and try a cup myself. I thought if I made it with a lot of milk it might be okay. It smelled great, looked disgusting and tasted even worse. A mug of that and I would have been wired enough to leap a tall building in a single bound.

Obviously I'm not a coffee drinker, or destined to be one. Probably just as well, given I can never figure out what all the various types are — latte flats or is it white lattes and flat macchiato? I do know what a cappuccino is — that's the one with all the froth and the dusting of chocolate on top. I'm told you can buy one that is just froth and chocolate. It's called a baby chino — which sounds more like a baby animal to me.

I've probably won my life share of magazine subscription prizes with the coffee maker but you never know so I'd best go send off the cheques for those other dozen magazines I want to subscribe to. One is offering a case of mixed wines. And yes, that's right. I don't drink wine either.

Confusion Reigns

I think I'm losing my mind. (Many would say it's long been lost!) Just as I was trying to decide whether it was the pre or post Christmas sales the stores were having, the Easter Bunny slipped in, waving Valentine's Day flowers and cards, bowled over Santa and took over the shelves. As I mistakenly thought Easter was around March or April I thought I'd lost a couple of months of the year somewhere.

If we've had Easter then Mother's Day must be coming up and as my daughter's birthday is the same month I'd better get cracking and organise her present, before we get overrun by the Father's Day merchandise — that must be just around the corner.

It's not just the stores that have me confused either. Once I thought footy was a winter sport and cricket was played in summer but we now have a footy grand final in March and cricket — well I guess it is summer somewhere in the world all year round. I'm waiting for the day they mistakenly schedule the two sports on the same oval on the same day. Will a batsman be out if they hit the footy umpire in the head with the cricket ball? The umpire will no doubt be 'out' anyway!

If it's possible to make matters worse, I find myself

wondering which country I'm actually living in. I always thought Halloween was an American custom but if so we have just become another US state. We've been tricked without the treat. I don't want a turkey in November. The only thanksgiving celebrations I want are when the house stays tidy for more than an hour and the cake tins stay full for more than five minutes.

I thought February was my birthday but suddenly find it is overrun by dragons and questions about whether it is the year of the pig or dog? In my case, more like the donkey I would say.

Enough is enough. We have International Days for just about everything on earth. I vote we have an International Day for putting everything back on the calendar where it darned well belongs.

By the way — it is only March, in case you wanted to know. Christmas has gone, Easter is on its way, Mother's Day is a couple of months off yet and Father's Day even further so sit back and breathe a sigh of relief. Just don't relax too much though — or you'll find yourself out looking for Christmas gifts next week.

Cook Wanted Urgently

One of the advantages of living in the middle of nowhere is that I am rarely asked to cook for cake stalls. My idea of the perfect fundraiser is the Cakeless Cake Stall. It doesn't involve any cooking at all; you just donate the cost of the ingredients. It is also a much safer option as my cooking failures are legendary.

At the age of fourteen my friend and I decided to make bread. We didn't make the yeast grow: we killed it — totally! Apparently there's just a little difference between the temperature of boiling water and tepid water! The resulting loaf of bread is probably still being used as a doorstop or maybe the cornerstone of a house, because it was certainly hard enough. The chooks bent their beaks trying to peck it and the dog didn't even attempt to chew on it.

Nevertheless for some odd reason my family actually likes my cooking and I am requested to make the same cakes and biscuits repeatedly. Yet after more than twenty years of using the same recipes I am still capable of leaving out vital ingredients. I've reinvented recipes by discovering what can be left out without making the end product totally inedible. Maybe I could make some money by selling them as *Raelene's Revamped Recipe Book*. I'm sure it would be a best seller (us writers are

renowned for our fertile imaginations).

I can make more mess when cooking than six pre-schoolers in the kitchen. My mother always said 'Clean up as you go,' and I always have good intentions but somehow it never happens. I'm sure Mum is watching from up above shaking her head and wondering where she went wrong. I swear ingredients and utensils dirty themselves while my back is turned. How else could one small batch of biscuits lead to so much mess and dirty dishes?

Quantities defeat me. If the recipe says it makes three dozen I'll be lucky to get one and half dozen or maybe two if I don't eat any mixture. If I try to double the size of a recipe it flops — now how can that be? Logic says if you put in double the ingredients you get double the quantity, so why does it never work for me? I look at people who churn out cakes and biscuits in quantities large enough to feed a shearing team and the family and wonder where I'm going wrong. I guess I just missed out on the cooking gene.

Cooking for visitors has a devastating effect on my cooking, as if it could get any worse. My most tried and true recipes stab me in the back. Cakes slump, biscuits sprawl, vegies soak the water dry and turn black. My specialty is Cremated Vegies!

My idea of heaven is when a visitor arrives and says, 'I love cooking. Would you like me to take over the kitchen?' I have to be careful not to scare them when I grab them with joy and squeeze until they are turning blue in the face. Before they can gather enough breath to run away I ask them if they'd like to extend their stay and stock the freezer while they are at it?

Five Star Disaster

I'm not sure what it is about me and conferences in flash city hotels. Every time I attend a conference there always seems to be a problem with the accommodation. Usually I share with a female friend but no matter what I say when booking we always end up with a double bed. As my friend said to one manager, 'We're close friends but not that close!'

At one Distance Education conference I managed to organise a room with single beds (not without an argument of course) only to find the beds were so close together that if one of us sneezed the other would be blown out of bed. Reorganising the furniture to give ourselves a little breathing, snoring and sneezing space solved the problem, or at least it did until we returned to our nicely made up room each night — there would be the beds cosily tucked up side by side again.

This hotel also managed to lose my suitcase for several hours and that was just between the lobby of the hotel and my eighth floor room. I was a little stressed since it contained all my clothes, most of them new, and my credit card wouldn't cope with any further demands on it. Fortunately it turned up, eventually, in another woman's room, but last I heard she was still looking for her case.

It's probably not considered the done thing but I always like to follow through on these slip ups. When my suitcase went missing I tried to phone reception to advise them but was unable to get through. So I traipsed down to the lobby to report a) the missing case and b) the faulty phone. A very obliging hotel clerk suggested I head back to the room where he would try ringing me to see if I was able to receive incoming calls. I duly did as I was told and waited patiently. A phone rang, but it wasn't coming from the instrument in the room, in fact it appeared to be coming from the bathroom. On further investigation I found the phone was indeed ringing in the bathroom, on the wall above the loo to be precise.

Now anyone will tell you I can talk anywhere, anytime, even underwater with a mouthful of marbles if they are being really unkind, but even I draw the line at talking on the phone while on the throne! There are some sounds people just do not need to hear over the phone.

Flower Arranging

I inherited my love of roses from my mother. My family don't share my passion — too often they have come off second best in an argument with the rose bushes, particularly my eldest son who is probably still traumatised from being catapulted in his walker head first into a rose bush as a toddler. The trauma may have had as much to do with the way his mother dragged him out again!

When my roses are blooming I occasionally get an urge to show them off in the house. Armed with secateurs I descend on the garden. If I didn't know better I'd say the rose bushes cower when they see me coming. I have no idea why. I cut and snip merrily, some yellow, some pink and definitely the mauve, all the while cursing the thorns.

Back in the house I trim stems while continuing to curse the thorns before I begin the search for the perfect vase which has to be the rose bowl that belonged to my mother, who, I might add, could put anything in a vase and make it look good.

Vase found, I gently (trying to avoid thorns) place roses in the vase, give them a wriggle and stand back to admire. Something isn't right. A few more wriggles, a tug at this one and a poke at that one (curse those damned thorns) and stand back for another look. Nope

— still not right so take them out and start again. Perhaps if I can arrange them flat on the table then I can pick them up and plonk them in the vase, they might look all right. Nice theory — does it work — NO! Still not right. Where's that darned garden book? What does it say about arranging roses — use warm water and pick early in the morning. Huh! Very helpful, it's nearly lunchtime and they have already been dunked in cold water half a dozen times.

I can do this. I will not be defeated by a bunch of flowers, no matter how beautiful (or vicious) they are. Back to square one. Take roses out of vase, trim some leaves off and try again, trim more leaves and those damned thorns. Finally I decide it must be the vase that is the problem, it's too tall — try the shorter one, well the rounder one then, that pot or the jug or that tin can.

My daughter comes in a little later with a bloom in her hand. 'Mum, why have you chucked all those pretty roses in the bin?' Maybe she will inherit my mother's flower arranging ability — it sure skipped a generation with me.

Food, Damned Food

'What's for tea, Mum?'

'Can we have scones for morning tea?'

'Is there any sweets tonight?'

'Is that cake all gone? Who ate the last piece?'

Sometimes I think my family's minds are eternally focused on food and their stomachs. I feel like I am running a feedlot for humans, where my role is to keep up a never ending supply of food to them. Even the chooks look like they're feeling short changed by the amount of scraps they are getting at present.

Not sure if the cold weather is to blame or if it is having the entire family at home — I'm sure it's not some miraculous improvement in my cooking flair — but as fast as I can buy, bake it or even burn it, they are devouring it. I stocked up at the beginning of the school holidays with enough food, I thought, to feed an army for a month. I realise now why they don't have growing boys full time in the army — they couldn't afford to feed them.

After my last shop I was pretty impressed with my fully stocked cupboards, pantry and freezer, almost smug, knowing there was no reason for anyone to complain there was nothing to eat in the house. A week later Mother Hubbard's dog wouldn't have even bothered going to the cupboard; he'd know the kids had long cleaned it out. I'm going to ask my son's boarding school if they feed him at all during the term, because judging by what he consumes in the holidays, it wouldn't seem like it. Not that he looks like he has been starved to death.

I thought I'd be clever and bake a super-size cake, doubling the mixture so it would last twice as long. Maths never was my strong point; they just ate it twice as quickly. The only way to keep any food in the cupboards is to make sure it's something they don't like. Baked beans will rust in the tin, low fat biscuits and other healthy fare last a while — until desperation sets in — and tomatoes only get eaten once they are turned into relish. It's not just the humans though. If I venture outside, the goats come running up for their food and the dog hovers like a blowfly, hoping for a handout.

I think I might hide for a while but before I do I'm going to have a look in the mirror — I'm sure there must be something like 'food supplier' tattooed on my forehead.

Green Fingers

From a distance my garden looks green and lush. It's only on closer inspection that the greenery turns out to be ninety percent weeds! Weeding is on my long list of pointless activities, along with cleaning, cooking and washing windows.

By the time I finish weeding one garden bed and think about starting on the next the first bed has a brand new crop of weeds. It could have something to do with the fact that my weeding attempts are sporadic, to say the least, for occasionally I do get the urge to weed and dig madly for half an hour or so. Fortunately the urge soon passes and is unlikely to bother me again for several months. And if I can ignore the urge for a day or so it soon goes away.

Weeds are the toughest plants in my garden. Nothing less than a deadly insecticide will kill them and even that doesn't always work. The dog waters them but that has no impact, nor does frost, heat or drought. If I could grow a crop that survives as well as my weeds I'd make a fortune and every farmer in Australia would be lining up to learn my secret.

Not only have I a large quantity of weeds but also an endless variety, with new ones arriving every year. I have flowering weeds, deep and shallow rooted weeds; weeds large and small, fat and thin. Some have quite pretty flowers and if you don't look too closely you could almost think they were meant to be in the garden.

Luckily the legitimate plants in my garden are very adaptable and have developed the ability to grow in and around the weeds. Often the weeds twine themselves through other plants, creating, in my eyes, quite an artistic display — though true gardeners may not agree! Sometimes I get a pleasant surprise when I discover a flower (whose existence I'd forgotten) poking its head up from amongst the feral weedery.

When I come to think of it, who says you can't have a garden consisting entirely of attractive and varied weeds? They grow profusely and easily, are hardy and difficult to kill, can be pruned quickly with a whipper snipper and some flower extravagantly. I could start a whole new trend in gardens for all us who don't have green thumbs.

The only problem is my husband, who does have a green thumb and prefers plants to weeds in our garden so I don't suppose he would be too impressed with my idea.

So I guess it is back to making the occasional attack on the weeds and continuing the search for long lost plants, hidden among the wilderness. Meanwhile I will continue to view the garden beds from a distance and enjoy the greenery.

It's a Weird World

Today in the schoolroom my daughter and I were discussing hoaxes and practical jokes, which led to looking up the Internet for weird facts that might be used in a hoax. Did I say weird? Some of these things go way beyond weird — beyond the super weird area. Whose job is it to find these things out anyway? Do people get paid to research this sort of information or are they just very curious? I'm not actually sure curious is the best word to describe them.

Apparently you can lead a cow upstairs but not downstairs. Now did they build a staircase in the paddock or just borrow someone's house? 'Excuse me, I was just wondering if I could bring my cow into your house and test my theory?' Luckily we didn't have stairs, so the question never arose. But I have a fair idea what my mother's response would have been after seeing her reaction when my brother put a foal on her polished back verandah.

We discovered that all polar bears are left-handed. Now come on! What did they do? Go up and shake hands? If I was close enough to a polar bear to check out what paw it was using I'd probably be a lot more interested in finding a way to put some serious distance between us. And you can't tell me they have checked every single polar bear in the world. There's got to be one polar bear out there who wants to be an individual.

A snail can sleep for three years! Hey, that's some hangover. How did they wake it up — was it like the sleeping princess and had to wait for someone to come along who wanted to kiss it? In that case it is probably still asleep! Who wants to spend three years of their life watching a snail to ensure it wasn't having them on and how do you tell if a snail is awake or asleep anyway, tucked away in their mobile home?

Elephants are the only animals that can't jump. Well thank goodness for small mercies. If elephants start jumping we're in trouble! Mother Nature obviously had some common sense when organising her animals. Mind you, there are other ways they could squash you, so best just keep out of their way.

A crocodile can't stick out its tongue. Well maybe it doesn't need to, it has other ways of showing it doesn't like you very much. Oh, and in case you try to grab its tongue and it tries to drag you under water, stick your thumbs in its eyes and it'll let you go. I wonder what muggins they got to test that theory.

And in the interests of health and safety and because I want you to be around to read some more of my writing, would you please take that pen out of your mouth. It is a known fact that, on average, one hundred people die each year from choking on a ballpoint pen!

Next time you are looking for some stimulating dinner party conversation look up some weird facts before you go. You are bound to gross out at least half the guests and cause an argument with the other half!

Hansel and Gretel

I recently cleaned my oven. Big deal I hear you say. But for me cleaning the oven is up there with a pap smear on the pleasure scale. When we bought the oven a couple of years ago I faithfully promised myself I would clean it after every use, so there would be no need for these marathon oven cleaning sessions over days.

The really silly thing is I would actually find the oven very easy to keep clean if only I didn't have to cook. No food in the oven equates to no spilt, sprayed or blackened matter inside and voila — no cleaning problem. Unfortunately my family seem to think cooking is part of my job description so the oven is going to get dirty occasionally, and cleaned — far less occasionally.

I'm beginning to think there is a gremlin hiding inside whose first mission it is to ensure the oven gets as filthy as possible. His second is to shower me with guilt every time I open the oven door and see how disgusting it is.

So there I was on my hands and knees with my head stuck in the oven door. Shades of Hansel, Gretel and the wicked witch, although she must have been a lot smaller than me — or Hansel and Gretel shoved really hard to squeeze her in.

I'd sprayed the entire inner surface the night before

with 'non caustic' oven cleaner. The only reason it's called 'non-caustic' is because it doesn't rip your skin off. It will still asphyxiate you if you dare to breathe while using it, but it will leave you with some skin.

It's funny, but you don't see too many ads on TV for oven cleaner — probably can't get any actor willing enough to risk life and limb trying to clean an oven and smile at the camera at the same time. She/he (let's not be sexist here) would have to be a contortionist at the least and a masochist as well.

After countless hours of scrubbing, choking, wiping, choking, rinsing, choking and reassembling (while choking) the job is done and as much as I hate to admit it there is a sense of satisfaction once the oven is clean. Those shiny silver trays winking at you convince you what a wonderful job you've done. It's almost enough to make you think about cleaning the oven regularly, if your lungs would stand up to another round with the 'non-caustic' cleaner.

A Taxing Time

While the pollies in Canberra fight over what tax break we'll get (negligible) and don't fight over the pay rise they'll get (more than generous), mere commoners like me are cursing the approaching 'end of financial year' mayhem.

For those super-organised superior beings who can't see what all the fuss is about, stop reading right now. You'll never understand. I promised myself twelve months ago (and twelve months before that) I'd file every bit of paper, write down every dollar earned (not many) and every expense (too many), keep receipts for every last thing and know exactly where they all are.

But somehow the receipts aren't in the receipt file, my beautifully ruled up cashbook has nothing written in it, and all my other paperwork has mysteriously disappeared. I just don't get it. The accountant keeps demanding I send him information, which requires more filing, more paperwork, more searching and usually a few more domestics.

And this is just for my personal taxation. If I had to do the station taxation as well, Peter Costello and John Howard wouldn't still be fighting over the leadership when I got around to that lot — they'd both be dead and buried.

I wouldn't be surprised to find the divorce rate soars around taxation time. Probably a lot of kids move out of home too, unless they are training to be accountants, in which case Mum and Dad will probably pay them to stay, providing they can sort out the tax mess.

This year I've got an additional complication to add to my tax income. I'm now the proud owner of a Super Fund, thanks to my appointment to a government board. An envelope stuffed with enough paper to have killed off at least half a dozen trees arrived by mail, congratulating me and telling me how to access my fund.

Imagine my excitement when I logged in to the account on the Net to find I had — wait for it — a grand total of eight dollars ($8) working for me there. Now that's what I call a retirement fund. By the time I hang up the typewriter I might have enough dosh to shout myself lunch, before I become a bagwoman and move onto the street.

Every time the powers that be tell us the tax system is getting simpler I get a sick feeling inside, because the 'simpler' they make it the more confused I get. Not sure if that says something about my lack of grey matter, but I think it says more about their use of the word simple. Actually I think I must be a bit simple to even believe them in the first place.

So be warned when they send you a simple tax form to fill in. Be prepared to set aside several days and hand over every detail of your life, right down to your undie size. Oh and be sure you've got the receipt for those undies — maybe they'll be tax deductible one day!

Washing Woes

I'm thinking of buying a laundrette. Not as a business, but so that each member of my family can have their own washing machine. It's the only way I can see to get over the mountain of washing that always fills my laundry.

The washing pile in this house grows faster than a major bank's profit margin. Several loads go through the machine in the morning and at the end of the day the wash basket is overflowing again.

Where does it all come from? It's not because my family are so incredibly clean they insist on changing their clothes every five minutes. In fact the men are happy to wear their clothes for several days regardless of whether they are held up by grease, mud or just good old red dirt.

Yet somehow the laundry mountain just keeps growing. If I wake up one morning with a fantasy playing out in my head of a washing-free day, you can be sure there'll be no clean tea towels or oven mitts and someone has spilt something on the last clean tablecloth.

I've tried hiding my laundry basket, or putting it out in the fresh air — maybe sunlight might kill off whatever gremlins are living in it and manufacturing washing —

but it hasn't worked so far. It's crossed my mind that perhaps the clothes get up to mischief and reproduce themselves in the laundry basket.

Even the washing machine has had enough and has threatened to go on strike more than once — waltzing across the laundry floor in an attempt to make a run for it and get a well earned break.

Sometimes I'm tempted to fold up the clean washing and hide it. If they can't find it they can't dirty it, right? Doesn't work though — I can hear the screams now: *Where's my jeans? Why haven't I got any clean socks? Who's pinched my shirts?* Mind you, I hear all this most days anyway.

Occasionally a miracle occurs and I can admire the empty washing basket as I smugly stroll past on my way to one of the children's bedrooms. Hang on — what's that awful smell coming from under that bed? Yep! You guessed it — more dirty washing!

Heard and Seen

Technology is getting out of hand. Now we have mobile phones that can do everything except iron your clothes (what a shame — that would be a winner with me). The one that daunts me the most though is the phone that has a video screen, so you and your caller can see one another as you speak.

The mind boggles, just imagine it. It's six in the morning and the phone rings. You crawl out of bed to find the phone or fall out of bed trying to reach it on the bedside table. Press the receive button and hey presto there's your caller looking bright, bubbly and beautiful. You, on the other hand, have a punk rock hair do, bleary sleep filled eyes and are still in your night attire, whatever that may (or may not) consist of. Not a pretty sight by any stretch of the imagination.

Some people might suggest that anyone ringing at uncivilised hours deserve to look at something resembling the wreck of the Hesperus but they aren't the ones hoping the caller, an editor based on Australia's east coast, is ringing to tell you they want to give you a regular paid position writing an exclusive column for their paper. They don't understand this time difference game and aren't going to be terribly impressed with the view of their prospective columnist.

Speaking on the phone without actually being seen by your caller has numerous advantages. You can tell little white lies like, 'I know exactly where that is, just let me grab the file,' while upending the entire contents of the filing cabinet onto the floor. They can't see if you're having a bad hair day, or haven't shaved your legs for a month, or you're wearing your daggiest trackies. Unseen, you can talk in your sweetest tones to the biggest bore in the world, while drawing instruments of torture on your doodle pad.

Departments that put you on hold for half a lifetime have no idea of the words you are scribbling down to describe them and their efficiency.

I don't think my callers need to know the state of my house or see the rude signals I am giving my kids to tell them not to interrupt; I also don't need to see what is happening at their end of the phone. If they have just spilt coffee down their shirt or are picking their nose — that's more information than I want.

Technology is a wonderful thing and I am one of its biggest fans but I feel sometimes we just need to keep a little of that 'mystique' that surrounds talking on the phone to someone you've never met. After all, if they want to imagine me as tall, slim and glamorous who am I to deprive them?

Legitimate Bush Woman

I don't spend much time getting around our property, which probably accounts for all the things I can't do and the rest of my family can.

Take our cattle for instance. (No I don't mean literally, that's stealing.) The hubby or sons will do a windmill run and return saying, 'That roan cow with the broken horn was at Tommy's Mill today,' or 'The steer we let go last year, out of the white cow, is back at Number Five.' There's only about four thousand head of cattle on the place and they can recognise individuals!

I can recognise two. One is known as Fat Cow, although now she's like a hat rack thanks to the drought and old age, while the other is Monique, named after a young jillaroo we had. I know her because she always has her head over the yard fence, eating my garden!

As for this business of telling the gender from a distance, I'm battling to know what sex they are unless I'm on my knees looking underneath them. Even then it's not always as obvious as you'd think, and I don't try too hard because it is a pretty vulnerable position to be in.

My kids can find their way around the property with eyes closed almost — though the youngest daughter still needs a bit of practice to catch up to her brothers. But

take me a kilometre from home, turn me around, and I'm completely, totally, miserably lost.

On my first attempt at mustering they told me to head north.

'How do I know which way's north?' was my plaintive cry.

'Just follow the plane,' I was tersely instructed.

'I can't see it; the sun's in my eyes.'

'Look out your right window and head that way.'

So I did, having absolutely no idea where I was headed. I just followed the cattle and hoped they knew which way they were going.

My husband now has a global positioning thingy. I'm not sure why — he isn't the one that continually gets lost. He could give the GPS to me except I wouldn't have the first idea how to use it and you probably have to know where you are in the first instance to be able to return there.

I'm afraid the writers of Mills and Boons would have written me off as a lost cause. No white moleskins, akubra and RM boots; hopeless at cooking and even worse at sewing. No gin and tonics under the stars at night and I can't change a tyre or fix a windmill for love or money.

Maybe if I'm around long enough, the husband and kids will finally manage to convert me into a legitimate bush woman, although I think after nearly a quarter of a century they have pretty much given up. However, one should never discount the possibility of a miracle, should one?

How's Your Concentration Span?

Last night I suddenly got the urge to do some knitting so I fossicked out some needles and wool. There is always something around from my many past attempts at actually completing a knitting project. Knitting always seems such a winter thing to do — feet up in front of the heater, needles clacking away and me full of enthusiasm and determined to actually end up with a finished item this time.

Naturally, as per the law that says, 'As soon as Mum sits down we have to know why and what for and how long for,' the kids all want to know what I'm making. Our conversation goes like this:

Number Three child: What are you making?

Me: I don't know. I'm just knitting.

Number Two child: But how can you knit if you don't know what you're knitting?

Me: Well I just knit until it turns into something.

Number Three child: Oh I know, you're making a scarf.

Me: Maybe, maybe not!

Number Three child: Well what else could it be?

Me: Maybe it will just be a square.

Number Two child: What's the use of one square?

Me: I might make a few squares and join them together.

Number Three child: Oh, like a rug.

Me: Well maybe, but if I get bored then I'll probably just unravel what I've done and roll the wool up again.

At this Number One son rolls his eyes and shakes his head. He's obviously decided his mother has finally succumbed to the complete madness that's been threatening for most of his lifetime.

That's the problem with having the attention span of a mosquito; you get bored with an activity very quickly. It's a bit like when I have the occasional brilliant idea to cook some fresh biscuits or cakes for the ravening horde. By the time I've thought of the idea, searched out a recipe for which I actually have (most of) the ingredients and recalled how to use the oven — I've lost interest. Mending is another activity that doesn't seem to be able to hold my attention for long, along with watching reality TV shows and listening to parents who think their child is the next Albert Einstein.

However before you go thinking I'm some empty-headed blonde, you should know I do have the ability to concentrate on the things in life that are really important — such as devouring a block of chocolate, reading a great book, booking my air fare for a trip away and spending money!

Jet Lagged

Can you get jet lag from interstate flights? It isn't the late nights, early mornings, chatting, working, sightseeing, eating and drinking that have worn me out — it must be jet lag!

I've just returned from a week in Sydney attending a conference for rural and remote parents and I took a few extra days for sightseeing. I saw the Blue Mountains, and they really are blue. I also saw some blue men and I wasn't drinking or taking drugs. They strolled up the main street of Sydney with their entire upper torso painted blue. Perhaps they were fugitives from a circus? I also saw kangaroos, emus and dingoes. Not in the main street of course, but at a wildlife park which I was really hanging out to visit in order to see all these exotic animals that are so foreign to me!

Sydney has double everything, including Double Bay, double decker buses, double decker trains and boats, and their drivers are at least as twice as mad as any I've ever experienced anywhere before. The horn is practically as vital to the car as the engine. The quickest revenue raiser for the New South Wales government would be to fine everyone for unnecessary 'tooting' — they'd raise a fortune. And it's the only place I've been where a taxi ride made me carsick!

I always though green lights meant 'go', amber meant proceed with caution and red meant 'stop' — that's what we were taught at primary school. Not in Sydney. Green means keep going, amber means step on it and go faster and red means stop only if you absolutely have to. I never crossed a road on foot unless I was tucked in the middle of a crowd for protection.

The hotel we stayed in was lovely once I figured out the various idiosyncrasies. Take the light switches, for instance: while four switches had to be pushed down, the fifth went up. The air con only worked when the magic card was in and the bathroom door had to be closed to give you room to sit on the loo.

I don't think they were quite prepared for the influx of bushies who were in town for the week and intending making the most of every moment. Closing the bar early in the evening elicited lots of protests before a mass exodus out to find an open bar. I think they may be used to a more refined guest in their hotel.

Now I'm home and back to reality. The credit card is bowing under the weight of what is owed on it, the body is suffering from jet lag as I said and school starts again tomorrow. Oh what a feeling! Hopefully I'll be well and truly recovered in time to set off again for next year's conference — some people just never learn!

Winter Woes

I woke up this morning and thought I must have been transported to Melbourne. It was overcast, cold and raining, the sort of morning perfect for lying in bed — except when you've got a column deadline breathing down your neck, or kids to get into the schoolroom.

I get a lot of flack around here if I dare mention being cold as I have made the grave mistake of saying how much I prefer winter to summer. So of course the minute I dare have a whinge about the cold weather I'm put very smartly back into my box — without a heater!

It's not that I'm so hard to please when it comes to the weather. I don't really want much. Shall we say, for autumn and spring to last more than a week or two and for summer to be about two months shorter and 25 degrees cooler.

Part of my problem I think is that my body thermostat seems to be completely skewed. I'm sweating it out when others are putting their jumpers on. When they decide it's warm enough for shorts and a T-shirt I'm almost ready to pass out. (You didn't think I was going to say go naked did you?)

There does come a point though when even I have to admit it's cold — it could be something to do with the icicles hanging off my ear lobes, to say nothing of the never-ending drip at the end of my nose, which threatens to freeze into an icicle also.

These are the days when I suddenly become the dedicated housewife and mother, slaving away over the wood stove in the kitchen. Could someone bring me more wood for the fire? The biscuits might burn if I leave them!

Of course if we are doing school then I need the heater on because I can't expect my child to work in a cold classroom now, can I? That would be too cruel and it is impossible to write with frozen hands. The fact that the heat flows through to my office next door is just an added bonus.

I haven't yet found the solution to frozen hands as I can't seem to type with gloves on, nor do I get much done with my hands in my pockets. Perhaps I'll just have to sit in front of the heater with a warm mug of Milo until my hands thaw out. I'm sure the editor will understand why this month's column is a tad late!

Let There Be Light

Us bush people appreciate modern facilities and technology more than our city cousins. Why? Because we haven't always had it, in fact some still haven't got it. So I understand when someone gets excited because they've got a fly wire door on their kitchen or a new loo, let alone a new loo with dual flush — now that's exciting.

When our friend, let's just call him Al, got solar power and, subsequently, a new electric fridge he was constantly opening and closing the door, not because his previous fridge didn't have a door but because it didn't have a light. And if you've ever had a fridge without a light you know what a novelty it is to open one that has a light and actually see what's in your fridge (even though sometimes you'd rather *not* know what's in there!).

And to make it even more exciting, Al's new fridge makes ice too. Now for all you cynics out there who say, 'Well duh, every fridge makes ice,' get back in your box — it isn't true! Try spending a summer in the bush with an old kero or gas fridge and see how much ice you get. Generally you're lucky to get your water cooler than tepid, let alone freeze. Iceblocks, ice cream and frozen foods are a luxurious dream.

I can relate to Al and his excitement over the new technology at his house.

After all I was the one who, when we first had our phone installed and it rang, ran around like a lunatic telling the family, 'It's the phone, it's ringing, it's the phone, listen,' until my husband kindly suggested I answer it. I've also been known to get excited over a new washing machine because it was large enough to wash all the sheets in one load.

The novelty factor of getting up in the night and switching on a light hasn't worn off yet. I still recall getting up to feed babies in the middle of the night when we had only generator power. Trying to light a gas lamp while holding a torch and a screaming baby was always fun, to say nothing of scraping dirty nappies into the loo with the aid of same torch — you had to hope your aim was good. Now, at least, if the kids are sick in the night you can turn on the light and be sure they know exactly where the bucket is.

Al has left the bush now and lives almost in suburbia. I wonder if he is still enjoying his 'lit up' fridge — I might ring him one day and ask. I have a funny feeling though that Al won't be telling me any more of his secrets if they are going to end up in print!

Press One, then Scream

There have been advertisements on TV recently showing a woman attempting to phone her bank manager but unable to get past the automated prompt system. I know exactly how she feels and I bet you do too.

Ever tried phoning a government department? My last attempt went like this. The first number was engaged for three days. I eventually found a different number. Success, it was ringing. Then that dreaded voice started. *If you wish to ... press 1, if you wish ... press 2*. After pressing numerous buttons I finally got through to the department I wanted. The voice began again. *This call may be monitored ...*

I'm now frustrated enough to start talking back. 'I don't give a continental if you monitor the call; just get someone to answer the darned thing.' Luckily I don't suffer from high blood pressure or angina because I'd be probably be on life support by now if I did. Finally the same disembodied voice says, *All our operators are busy. You have been placed in a queue and your call will be attended to as soon as possible.* I've lost count of how many times I've heard this message before I give up.

Now I don't mind being in a queue in the supermarket because I can see how long the queue is, I can usually find someone to talk to, there are magazines to browse and I can see the queue moving. Sometimes these 'ghost voices' tell you how long the queue is that they have left you dangling in, but rarely. Let's face it if I'm in tenth place then maybe I'll consider hanging around but if there are 297 others in front of me I'm giving up right now.

Even more infuriating is when you are halfway through pressing never-ending buttons only to discover you pressed the wrong number and have to go back and start all over again. It's more frustrating than a game of snakes and ladders where you keep going down the snakes and your five year old beats you in about ten moves.

Imagine if just once the ghost voice got the message wrong and said, *I am connecting you directly to the person you wish to speak to, do not press any buttons. What state are you in so I can connect you to someone in your own time zone?*

Think how many millions of dollars would be saved by people not having to take stress leave because they go around all day saying 'press one, press two' or the number of phones that aren't hurled around rooms or ripped off walls. On the other hand there may be an increase in ambulance call outs for people suffering shock when their call is answered by a living, breathing human being.

Horses on Courses

Who says gambling on horse races is a mug's game? Not me! I won $11 at the Meeka races. Don't knock it — $11 will buy a couple of blocks of chocolate. (Hah! You thought I was going to say beer! When did you last buy a block of beer?)

Just follow my very professional method and hey presto you're a winner.

Step one: Study the race form guide — that's the book filled with all sorts of information you won't understand. Don't worry about that — it's all irrelevant. All you need to look at is the list of horses' names and choose one that takes your fancy. Also, you should check the colours the jockey wears too, make sure it isn't a colour you wouldn't be seen dead in.

Step two: Head for the Tote — don't worry if you don't know what that is or where it is — just follow the crowd. When you get to the head of the queue wave some money at the person inside and in your best I-know-what-I'm-doing voice say, 'Five dollars (I'm a big gambler) on Sticky Joe.' You also have to say whether you want to bet for a win or place — a win you get more money, a place you get less money. That's all you need to know.

Step 3: Stroll to the mounting yards which will be full of horses and little short men being given instructions by serious looking men and women. Once you spot your horse by the number on the cloth under its saddle, check it looks to be half awake, has four legs, a head and tail and isn't trying to kill its trainer or jockey. If so, things are looking good.

Step 4: Shove your way politely (or, if that doesn't work, standing on a few toes helps) to the fence to watch the race, most of which you won't be able to see until they actually run straight past you, by which time you've probably forgotten what the horse looked like and its number, anyway. Don't worry — just watch until they bring the winning horse into the saddling yard and put it into the number one enclosure, at which point you can check its number to determine if you've backed the winner.

Step 5: Naturally, after all that precise work your chosen horse will have come in a winner, and oh so casually (it's not done to dance and shout your good fortunes to all and sundry) you need to follow the crowd again — the ones that are smiling and happy, not the grumpy ones throwing tickets on the ground — and collect your winnings.

Step 6: Join all the other winners and enjoy a celebratory drink before starting all over again.

If you ever get to the Meekatharra races look out for me — I'm the one shaking coins out of my money box for my next big bet. Do stop by and say hello and I'll be happy to give you my hot tips.

The Ultimate Revenge

Bras are a conspiracy against women. They were obviously invented by men who knew full well that their male counterparts wouldn't have to wear the damned things. In fact I think the original male inventor was probably using it as payback against a lady friend who had upset him rather badly. Either that or she was so well endowed he invented it out of concern for his own safety?

Bras were designed to turn women into contortionists. If you put them on so the front is at the front (makes sense, one would think) you could dislocate both shoulders trying to do them up. So you put them on back to front and remove a layer of skin dragging them round the right way. Those glamorous maternity bras do up at the front but if you're not lactating you're out of luck with front fasteners.

And whose brainwave was it to add the piece of fencing wire? How many repairmen have fished those little instruments of torture from within the internal parts of a washing machine? How many women have found a wire creeping up under her armpit at the most inopportune moments in life? I actually had a collection at one point in time as I kept thinking a) I'll put them back in the bra or b) that wire could be useful one day. I didn't and they weren't.

Women didn't burn their bras because of the feminist movement; they just hated wearing the damned things. I'd happily burn mine but gravity means it is safer for me and everyone else if I don't.

Right from the start us girls get the raw end of the deal, beginning with being fitted for a training bra. A what? How do you train a bra or is it what the bra contains that we are training and what would we be training them to do? Why don't boys have training jocks so they can learn to politely and discreetly arrange or adjust the contents?

Being fitted for bras is the ultimate humiliation process. Some snooty saleswoman sidles up and says, 'What size cup are you dear?' What are we talking here? Eggcups, coffee mugs or maybe a thimble?

'Just poke that bit in, dear, now give them a little shake. Mmmmm, maybe a size larger!' Did I say coffee mug? More like mixing bowl.

Next time my husband wants some jocks I'm not buying them. I'm going to drag him to the store, insist a male salesperson accompanies him into the fitting room and makes him try them on. The salesman will make it as difficult as possible to get them on, perhaps by insisting he drag them down over his head. Then the salesperson will say in his loudest voice, 'Hmm, not much there Sir, perhaps a size or two smaller.'

That's what I call revenge! Dream on.

One for the Birds

'Raindrops keep falling on my head!' Well actually they're not but something else might be shortly.

For some years now a pair of swallows have decided we are really nice people and they'd like to be part of our family. The first year they happily built a nest and hatched their babies while we watched in fascination. The babies thrived and we laughed at their kamikaze attempts to fly and said 'aren't they cute' and occasionally noted how much poop such little birds could excrete.

What we didn't realise was that they intended on becoming permanent residents — we thought they were just visiting for a season. We tried discouraging them by removing their nests before they started playing happy families but these guys had never heard of Industrial Relations. They just kept on building and rebuilding.

This year we kept a close eye on them, ready to deconstruct the minute they started to construct but it appeared we were no longer flavour of the month and they moved house anyway. I was quite relieved because it really did feel quite heartless to tear down their home the minute they began work.

One warm day, with winter on the decline, I decided

to clean out the 'summer residence' — otherwise known as the bough shed or cool house. This is a large construction with walls made of wire containing wads of spinifex. A water pipe drips water down the walls creating a lovely cooling effect when the wind blows. It can also create the effect of a sauna when the wind doesn't blow but that's another story. We use it as our siesta place during the heat of summer afternoons, and used to have lunch there before we got the air con in the kitchen.

After a few months of winter and no one using the bough shed it always needs an intensive spring clean. On entering, the first thing I spied was one of our swallow friends sitting happily on a roof beam. In the corner of the roof, right above my bed, was the other half, happily ensconced in a designer nest.

Now, when I'm asleep I'd like to think my mouth wasn't gaping wide open, and as I know I most definitely do not snore (not sure what my husband and kids are sniggering about), then I shouldn't have any cause for concern. But even the very thought of something small, wet and sloppy falling anywhere on my face or body makes me think of grabbing for a bucket, so I think there is going to be a showdown.

However this time they were too clever for me. Somehow they knew I don't have any head for heights and their nest was well out of my reach, even with a broom or other weapon in hand.

A bird in the hand is supposed to be worth two in the bush. Not sure why — I'd rather they were all in the bush!

Relaxing at the Dentist

A friend told me the other day she had gone to sleep in the dentist chair. Now that takes some doing. I always knew she was strange, this just proved it! I'm about as likely to sleep in the dentist's chair as I am to decide I want a snake for a pet.

The smell of the dentist's surgery alone keeps me awake. My eyes are always closed so I can't see the instruments of torture. That evil looking needle that could pierce a cow's hide, the hook that will attempt to drag my teeth out of my head or the pavement pounding drill used to grind through my teeth and into my skull.

If I even think about relaxing for one brief second, I hear the dreaded words, 'Wider please, just a little wider.' What does he think I am — one of those snakes that can disconnect its jaws to swallow a human whole? If I was I know who the first human in my sights would be!

And another thing, I'm amazed the dentist stopped talking long enough for her to go to sleep. Why do dentists insist on trying to talk to you while your mouth is full of instruments? They like to ask questions like, 'Are you okay?' You can't nod because of the headlock the dentist has on you so you try to say 'Yes,' which comes out sounding like the noise a choking cat would make. Some cruel people, supposedly my friends, would tell you I can talk underwater, but with a mouthful of dentist's metal — even I admit defeat.

Then there's the wonderful rinse and spit routine to look forward to. You have no control over your mouth so the rinse becomes a dribble and the spit — which you try to mop up with the disposable bib tied round your neck — stretches from the basin to your mouth.

After-dentist outings are fun too. The dentist gives you strict instructions as to what you can and can't eat/drink and how often. Chewing doesn't seem to be an option in case you chew your own cheek off so you opt for soup, which you have to leave until it is lukewarm. You gently spoon it into one side of your mouth only to find it is dribbling back out the other side.

Be warned, if you happen to be out with your children and this happens they will disown you, loyal people that they are. Never mind the years you've spent cleaning them up, at both ends!

Sleeping Beautifully

I was dead chuffed when a friend once called me 'a legitimate bush woman'. What an impressive title, I thought, and she wasn't even being ironical. Sadly though I think I may have to relinquish it as I may be using it under several counts of false pretences.

My lack of qualifications for the title includes my famous dislike of camping, especially sleeping in swags. I like my bed clean, comfortable and permanent. Despite my generous supply of natural padding, I find a swag on the ground about as comfortable as lying on a bed of nails. I toss and turn all night, never mind what the expert 'bushies' tell you about making a small hollow for your hip and you'll sleep like a baby — it doesn't work. Either that or this baby has chronic colic. If I can put my swag on a bed then I'm a little happier although I find the bedding tends to go AWOL during the night so that in winter I wake up freezing and in summer I find the mosquitoes have opted for my body as the chosen site of their annual picnic.

However there are times when one just has to suffer for the cause and such times include attendance at School of the Air camps. Recently my daughter and I attended a school camp and as she doesn't yet own a swag her brother's was called into service. From past experience I knew it would be wise to unroll and check the swag contents before taking it to camp, in order to wash several months of dirt and smoke from the bedding, remove the sticks and prickles and check no friendly critters were still lurking inside. After that I then checked my own swag, which is usually in pristine condition thanks to my efforts to avoid using it whenever possible. I made it up with clean sheets, a warm doona, my pillow and a spare blanket or two. By the time I got all that in and rolled it up it barely fitted in the car.

We packed what space remained with the other bits and pieces required for a camp of less than a week — clothing, schoolwork, vegetables from the garden surplus to our requirements, water (can't stand that town water), food and other essentials such as several blocks of chocolate for late night parent discussions.

On arrival at camp imagine my glee at discovering not only a bed, but one already made up with mattress, linen, doona and pillow, ready and waiting for me.

Now that's what this Legitimate Bush Woman calls 'camping with class!'

Roughing It

As far as camps go it's five stars all the way, not like the good old days. This time I'm sleeping in a bed, not a swag. It has linen I don't have to wash. The bathroom has constant hot water and there are only five of us sharing it. We only need to buy supplies one day at a time instead of for the whole week.

Once, at any school camp I was involved in, the height of luxury was two showers for the whole camp and a loo that didn't block up before the week was over. There was no popping down to the shop, so when a child decided to test how much paper could be shoved down one toilet, there was a real sense of urgency about getting further supplies.

Those with the acquired skills of log chopping (we quickly learn who not to mess with) were delegated to boiler duty — no wood: no fire: no hot water. Camps were guaranteed to fall into line with the coldest nights of the year so a hot shower was a necessity for thawing out, if not for cleanliness. The children were showered very rapidly, usually a few at a time, in order to ensure hot water was left for the mums/teachers/governesses.

The cooking regime started before you even left home, baking a supply of biscuits and cakes for smokos, plus a casserole for tea on the first night, and it never let up for the whole week — feed them, wash up, prepare the food, feed them ... Fridges were often hit and miss with doors that didn't always close properly thus ensuring all food had to be given a thorough inspection before being cooked or dished up. With stoves you could be lucky with a relatively new gas range, but it could just as easily be an old wood-burning stoves that took three trees just to cook a roast.

On returning home from camp — tired, grubby and with one or more equally tired and grumpy kids — you swear that is the last camp you are ever attending in your lifetime. Your husband's complaints on your arrival — no food in the cupboard and his lack of clean clothes — are usually met with a reaction that makes him very aware that your interest in his problems is lower than the proverbial snake's belly. Not too many husbands make that mistake twice — they're too scared that when the next camp comes around they would be the one packed off with kids, swags and food for a week of 'rest and relaxation'.

The good old days they might have been, but give me this new style of school camp any day!

Christmas Fare

I was talking to a friend the other day and she said she was running late making her Christmas pudding. It was still only July! I smiled sweetly and mumbled something as I snuck away. It's not too late for me to organise mine either — if the store hasn't got the ones in the plastic containers you heat in the microwave they've got plenty of time to order them in!

As far as I can recall I've never made a traditional Christmas pudding. I used to cook the occasional steamed fruit pudding but the novelty of that soon wore off. By the time I'd boiled half a dozen dry and drowned the next few with water seeping in under the lid, I'd decided not to waste my time or raise my family's hopes again. If I made one these days it wouldn't be good for the family's health, not because of cholesterol or the high calorie count — just the shock of me actually cooking one would do them in.

As for Christmas cakes, I've always felt it was important to support worthy organisations such as the Lions Club who do a very nice Christmas cake and you can always pour some more rum, whisky or brandy over it to say that you really did have a hand in making it.

I did make a Christmas cake once. It was in the early

heady days of marriage when I did all the housewifely things like cooking, cleaning and baking (what was I thinking?). I found a recipe for a Christmas cake, bought the ingredients, baked the cake and admired the result. I was very proud of my efforts and every few days would unwrap it, pour a little more 'body' over it and wrap it up carefully again. That year it was our turn to visit my parents for Christmas, so with cake carefully packed we headed south.

My parents had arranged for us to catch up with some friends just after Christmas, so I decided this was the perfect time to unveil my piece de resistance and prove to my mother, once and for all, that I could cook! (She seemed to have a lot of doubts in this area.)

With everyone eagerly awaiting a piece of the much lauded cake I carefully peeled off the alfoil I'd preserved it in, only to discover there was enough mould growing on the cake to start my own penicillin factory. I was mortified, everyone else was hysterical with laughter, and the chooks presumably had a very merry Christmas. They wolfed back every last crumb anyway.

I couldn't fathom it. All that sugar and alcohol should have made the ultimate preserving agents. If anyone can explain this to me, I'd be very pleased to hear from you. Not that I have any intention of ever attempting another Christmas cake. I don't believe, 'If at first you don't succeed try again.' More like 'Why try when you can buy?'

Send in the Robots

I once returned from a trip to the city with two new vacuum cleaners —a major case of overkill, you might think, for someone who uses a vacuum cleaner so rarely that my original one lasted twenty years.

The reason for buying two cleaners was simple: a large one for the large jobs, and a small one for the minor jobs. This is a woman's logic at work. Men wouldn't understand because in their eyes no matter how small the job is you have to have the largest and most impressive tools to complete it.

The new vacuum cleaners were put in the office where they quite happily sat for many months without being used. I have an intense relationship with vacuum cleaners — I intensely hate vacuuming. It is never a straightforward process for me. Firstly I always have trouble working out which lever to push for carpet and which for bare floors. I only need the one for bare floors, but should the little sweeper doodads be up or down? While in operation, the cord tangles itself around everything and the cleaner always turns itself over in a turtle impersonation and lies there upside down unable to right itself. Then you need a degree in rocket science to reassemble it after emptying the bag.

I am waiting impatiently for the day when you buy a vacuum cleaner and it comes complete with robotic controls. You just have to punch in the instructions: 'Vacuum all floors, search back of lounge for hidden treasures such as pens, toys and crumbs and finish by sucking up all spider webs complete with spiders.' When it has completed its list of chores it would then wind up its own hoses, gather up its myriad attachments and neatly put itself away in the cupboard.

Am I being unrealistic? I don't think so. Look at the what the scientists have come up with so far, fridges that allow you to check your emails, air conditioners that can adjust their own temperatures, cars that tell you where to go, and a washing machine that can give you instructions (without swearing like I do at times!).

I'm looking forward to the day of automated households when I sit back in the lap of luxury as my every wish and command is carried out by technological tools or automated robot. My husband and children would probably tell you that happens now: it's just that they are standing in for the robot!

Sounds of Silence

There's only one reason I'm writing this column early on a Sunday morning. Mozzies. No, I don't have trained mozzies with whips chasing me to the computer to meet my deadline. Just that their high-pitched whine and dive-bombing manoeuvres while obviously practising for an aerobatic display finally got too much for me. I hope they all end up having accidents and falling out of the sky.

I don't mind sleeping outside in summer but if you have any illusions about the romantic silence of bush nights forget it. If it is dry the flies take on the 'wake up the world' duty. Hiding under the sheets prevents them getting in your ears or up your nose but it doesn't shut them up. Once there has been a bit of rain they hand over the baton to the mosquitoes who, at some ungodly hour each morning, arrive to buzz around our heads and sink their fangs into any bare bit of flesh they can find.

However it isn't only during the early mornings that the bush chorus can be heard. We had a friendly boobook owl around here for several weeks. At first it was all very novel and we'd listen out for it each night, but hearing *mopoke* over and over without pause soon lost its novelty and had us cursing as we tried to get some sleep. If I could have found the darned thing it would have got more than a *mopoke*, it would have been a darned *big* poke.

Should we be lucky enough to get a decent fall of rain the bullfrogs in the house creek awaken in the early evening and the choir master has them practising for endless hours to achieve the ultimate bullfrog 'We are Alive' chorus. I'm not sure how many of them are there but it sounds like thousands of two-stroke motors revving up and while we too are happy about the rain, I wish they could celebrate a little more discreetly.

As if that wasn't enough we also have a visiting bowerbird who imitates cats screeching; the cicadas favourite home is the tree right outside our bedroom window; and on occasions a lonely bull likes to sing us a lullaby. And if by some chance nature decides to have a quiet night, one of the kids is bound to start talking in their sleep.

I'm heading to the city for some peace and quiet.

Freddo's in a Jam

One of my first introductions to station life was sharing the shower with frogs. Not one or two but hundreds of them, sitting and staring at me from every surface. I'd stand in the middle of the shower, trying to keep an eye on all of them at once in case they decided on a mass attack. I had some of the briefest showers of my life during that time.

Frogs and I will never be close friends but these days I am very brave and will simply remove any I find wandering the house. I even allow one to live behind the toilet cistern, providing it (she? he? how can you tell?) only pokes its head out occasionally. Don't tell anyone, but I've even been known to have a conversation with it — it gets lonely out here sometimes! However the minute I find Freddo on the seat when I sit down, his days are numbered. If he doesn't die from being sat on (99% chance I'd say) then he'll be copping a squirt of pine-o-clean (that's not what you thought I was going to say, is it?), which will very quickly send him to 'froggy heaven'.

I still refuse to touch them though, due to their delightful habit of releasing their bladder the moment they come into contact with something — usually part of me — so removing them involves putting something between my skin and theirs, which preferably will contain them

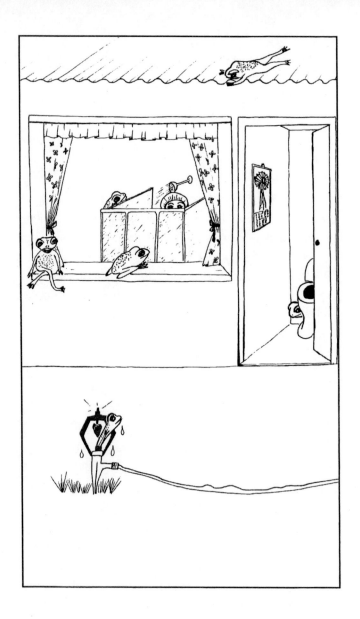

until I've tossed the frog back into the outside world.

Frogs outdoors don't usually bother me — unless they're doing their bladder trick on me. But I do have a problem with those frogs that insist on living in our sprinkler heads. Obviously it is a nice cool, wet spot and they think it is a lovely home. The problem starts however when the sprinklers are turned on. I have a habit of turning on the sprinklers without checking the head for residents.

Think about it. When a powerful jet of water moves through the hose and up into the sprinkler head, it doesn't leave anywhere for the frog to go other than up and out. Except sprinkler heads aren't designed for frogs to fit through. End result is one blocked sprinkler and one mangled frog, half in and half out of the sprinkler head.

Off comes the sprinkler head and on a good day out pops Freddo, none the worse for wear. On a bad day though, Freddo isn't going anywhere without my help and it is then I realise why I never wanted to go in for any form of medicine.

Once the sprinkler head is clear it's all systems go until I realise that perhaps it wasn't just a case of a frog in the sprinkler head, but a family of them lined up in the hose, because once again there is only a trickle of water and soon enough some froggy legs are waving at me from the beleaguered sprinkler.

Maybe I should invite some medical students to visit. They could practice their dissecting techniques and I could get on with watering my lawns.

By the way, if you're serving frog legs for dinner don't bother inviting me!

Stretch One, Two, Three

Who needs to sweat it out in a gym or twist and turn yourself inside out during aerobic classes? One good bout of grocery shopping every couple of weeks is guaranteed to tone up the muscles, including all those you didn't know you had, and get the heart pumping blood around your body like an Olympic sprinter.

Start off with some aerobic leaps to reach items on higher shelves but don't bring the entire shelf contents down on your head. This is best done wearing flat shoes. In high heels you could do yourself, or anyone around, you a serious mischief. I have it down to a fine art — take a flying leap into the air and swipe widely in direction of required item. Hopefully it lands in your hands or the trolley, and not on the head of the person behind you. It's not pretty, nor is it graceful, but generally it is quite effective. And it provides quite good entertainment for other shoppers.

Once your trolley has more than three items in it your arm muscles will get a thorough workout trying to steer it where you want it to go. No matter which direction you want your trolley to head it will try to pull you in the opposite direction. As you increase the quantity of items in the trolley you'll feel like you've got weights on the end of each arm.

With all shopping in the trolley it's time to head to the checkout for your waist bends. Up and down, out of trolley, onto checkout, out of trolley onto checkout — you know the routine! Don't forget to breathe while doing this, along with chatting to the cashier, saying 'no' to your children and apologising to the lady behind for your excess trolley load.

Move to other end of the checkout and start weight lifting. A bag with two kilos of sugar, four kilos of flour, six tins of dog food in one hand and a carton of drink in the other should have those arms looking in great shape in no time at all. The bum workout comes with shoving the shop door open and flexing the buttock muscles while you try to hold on to your trolley in the car park and prevent it from ramming every car you try to get past unscathed. You get a second (or is that the third?) bicep workout as you load grocery bags (or individual items if bags have broken) into the car.

Try to catch your breath while driving home because you aren't finished yet. You have to do all of the above in reverse until finally everything is stacked away in the pantry and fridge. Pat yourself on the back for an excellent workout before collapsing in a chair with a magazine and a coffee.

When the kids waltz in, open the cupboard or fridge and say, 'Isn't there anything to eat in this place?' that's your cue to give your lungs a really good aerobic workout!

Technology Traumas

Technology doesn't scare me — much. I can use a computer, a printer, and a scanner. I can turn the TV and stereo on and off, I can put a video in the recorder and I know I will work out how to use the DVD we got for Christmas too — given time.

I just need to wait until the kids are out of the way so I can find the manual and figure it out slowly, step by step. Of course I could just ask the kids to show me, but there is something very depressing about a ten year old giving you lessons on how to do something, it feels like the natural balance of parent/child goes out of whack.

'Can I have a turn now?' I plead in my best begging voice, learned from my experience with three children. 'No,' says my darling child, 'you're too old, you might break it!' It's scary how much that sounds like me.

It never pays to admit to your kids you that can't do something. The look of disbelief on their faces is too demoralising, and leads to me telling little fibs. 'Of course I never had any interest in it anyway,' or 'I could do it if I really wanted to do but I just can't be bothered.' The withering look I get following that is even more demoralising and requires at least half a block of chocolate to effect a full recovery.

DVDs seem to be a backward step to me anyway. I was watching one yesterday (yes, I got one of the kids to put it on for me) and stopped it before it was finished. When I went back to watch the last bit it went right back to the beginning. Now how daft is that? Any fool machine should know I don't want to start from the beginning. I pushed every button I could find on the remote but no luck. It was a far cry from my first television experience when my mother turned off the set halfway through a program I was watching. I was totally perplexed to find when she turned it back on that the program had disappeared. Maybe I was a very advanced child who was actually looking ahead to video/DVD technology!

I really want to see the end of this DVD, preferably without having to resort to asking the children to organise it all for me again. First I need to find where they hid the instruction manual (they said I'd stuff it all up if I tried to use it). Then get the lounge room to myself for an hour or three and figure it out, and I'll be kicking back with a self satisfied smirk enjoying the pleasures of DVDs at my command.

The question is, will the library give me an extended extension on the DVD loan? Maybe I should just stick to videos — or I could get the projector and slides out — the kids don't know how to use that!

The Family Tree

I recently attended a rellie bash in honour of my uncle's eightieth birthday. As he is one of ten children, of whom nine married and had children who have now had children and those children are having children — well you get the picture. The branches of the family tree are spreading far and wide and in many cases sagging quite badly with the weight of fruit!

It was a bit daunting to walk in and realise that 98 percent of the guests were relatives. My husband had the same long-suffering look on his face he always gets when we go to any of my rellie events. He thinks it is impossible for me to drag any more family out of the woodwork for him to meet but somehow I always do. As one of the youngest of all the cousins, and one who sees relatively little of the rest of the family, I am always a bit stuck about where everyone fits in. Combine that with my notorious ability to forget names five minutes after being told them and you can imagine some of the problems I have at such a gathering.

Fortunately I knew the guest of honour and his family quite well so I could whisper, *Who's that? Who do they belong to? Oh so that's Freddy's daughter — no Freddy's brother's daughter's child. Right! Got it!* Or maybe not because five minutes later I will have no idea and be calling them by the wrong name again.

With delight I spy a cousin who cannot be mistaken for anyone else because she is an exact replica of her mum and I knew that aunty very well. With a big smile and hug I greet her by name, only to discover I have the wrong sister! Well it was close — at least she was of the same parents.

Some cousins have been to stay with us at the station and of course they greet me with stories about their wonderful visits to my outback home while I'm frantically trying to remember said visit and nod blindly as they detail all the fun things we did while they were there.

The only solution I can see to being able to place my relatives better is to have more functions and get together more often. If I can refresh my memory more frequently I might not look like such a dill. For some reason my hubby looks a bit stunned when I suggest this idea though — can't imagine why!

Do You Know What You're Missing?

People are often shocked when I tell them I do a lot of my shopping on the Internet. They say things like, 'But you might get ripped off,' or 'I wouldn't have the patience,' and my all time favourite, 'But you don't get to visit all the shops.' They think I'm missing out on some wonderful retail experience.

After a recent trip to the city I discovered exactly what I've been missing.

On the Net you don't get to drive endlessly around car parks looking for a free space, and when you've finally found it discover in fact there's some miniature car hidden away in there.

Drivers don't wave with two fingers, toot their horns in a Christmas tune or wave vigorously at you when you're on the Net. Nor do you hear all the happy Christmas greetings they extend to you if you take more than five seconds to park.

There's not the fun of playing dodgem cars with shopping trolleys, trying to avoid crashing into others while protecting your own shins and running scared at the sight of children running loose with miniature trolleys or aggressive adults with full size ones.

And all the sounds of tinny Christmas carols being drowned out by screaming children, beeping scanners, cursing humans and the jolly Ho Ho Ho of a would be Santa who forgot his costume. There is no one spruiking at me to buy this or that — I really miss that.

Let's not forget the fun of a lunch break in the food hall where it appears every man, woman and child has congregated to buy something that looks like food, smells like food but actually it tastes like cardboard and is eaten at tables that Alice in Wonderland must have used her magic shrinking potion on. I really miss that when I'm sitting in the sun with my feet up and sipping on a fresh cup of tea and a home made scone, with all my shopping done and no parcels to worry about.

What sane person would want to miss out on the fun of queuing at the express checkout (I am curious as to how they define 'express' in these establishments) where you will only wait twenty minutes as opposed to the forty-five minutes in any other aisle, only to realise you have too many items and have to change checkouts anyway?

I'm humbled that people care enough to worry about what I am missing out on and the risks I face by shopping on the Internet. I care about them too so when they return from the shops stressed and hysterical I'll calm them down with a cup of tea, before I show them how to shop, stress free, kid free, noise free and traffic free — via the Internet.

The Invasion

Just how many insects are there in this world and why do they all want to live in my house? They've all moved inside instead of staying outside where all self-respecting creepy crawlies belong — someone obviously forgot to tell this lot or they've been brainwashed into thinking that my house is the Hyatt of insect hotels.

Take the grasshoppers for instance — really, feel free, take the whole darned lot if you like. What on earth is the attraction of my kitchen? I'm sick of fishing them out of the dishwashing water, trying to prevent them committing suicide by jumping into the microwave and seeing them fried when they land on the gas burner. They manage to make me feel guilty when I spray the flies (Flies! — well there's another whole column on its own!) and they do their death dance all over the place. I never thought I'd find myself apologising to a half dead grasshopper or putting it outside in the hope that the fresh air might revive it.

While not strictly in the insect category — they still fit in the creepy crawly scientific classification that I use — spiders are another of my pet hates. Not because I am terrified of them (much), but because they spin a web in every crevice, corner and space of the house that they can find. As fast as I can remove the webs they begin again. I'm sure they see me coming and prepare to move house. 'Oh-oh girls, here she comes. You go out the back and find a new spot for our next web. I'll sacrifice myself for our cause. If by chance I survive I'll join you shortly and we'll have that new web made before she can say 'damned spiders.'

Of course insects, like all of nature's creatures, have various bodily functions and if I was of a more scientific mind I could describe to you precisely what passes through the internal organs of the various insects, down to the quantity, shape and colour. As I'm not then I will just say that cleaning toilets is one thing; cleaning your walls and ceilings because insects use them as a toilet is another matter altogether.

As it is summer the insect population has increased about a hundredfold, particularly at nights and in the vicinity of lights. Somehow, in their eagerness to swarm around the light, they manage to squeeze inside the light shades too, so as summer rolls on and the insect graveyard expands, the lights get dimmer and dimmer. Eventually it will move me enough to empty the shades. The insects presumably think that is my way of making more of them welcome.

It has crossed my mind that perhaps the balance could be restored by me moving out of the house and leaving it to the insects. I could just crawl under some damp leaves somewhere — it's possibly cooler there anyway!

Murphy Strikes Again

I'm not sure what our family has done but whatever crime we've committed, Murphy's Law is doling out justice in spadefuls at our house lately. For those of you who don't know, Murphy's Laws states that 'Whatever can go wrong will go wrong — and at the worst possible moment.'

My computer has developed a mind of its own and shuts down at will, refusing to start again until it is ready. I think someone has been downloading Industrial Work Laws and the computer thought the information applied to it. I did dust and remove cobwebs but that wasn't enough to cure it. I won't be responsible for my behaviour if it dies completely and I have to survive without email/internet for any longer than a day.

The washing machine thought about dying but thankfully seems to have made a rapid recovery after being told it was headed for the dump. I've no doubt it is just biding its time though — until it's full of soaking wet, heavy towels for instance — to quit for good. It still gets a bee in its bonnet occasionally and waltzes across the laundry floor. Just as well it is attached to an electrical cord or I'm liable to find it making its way down the passage and out the door one day.

Taking its cue from the washing machine the hot water system decided to get in on the act and spring a leak. At first the washing machine got the blame (maybe that's why it was sulking?) until it became obvious that empty and off duty, the washing machine couldn't continually pour water on the laundry floor. One new hot water system coming up and one very wet floor until it arrives and hopefully no one will get electrocuted in the meanwhile. Should I suggest painting the laundry prior to the changeover? If I value my life, it might be an idea to leave that otherwise excellent suggestion out of the equation for now.

The power system isn't blameless in all this chaos either. Like everything else solar power is wonderful when it works. At the moment power to the house suddenly dries up for no apparent reason — the inverter is on, batteries are charged and the sun is shining. Today it went one step better. We lost only some of our power, this time a faulty fuse at the house was to blame. Of course there is no electrician or solar expert within phone reach, let alone available to drop in and investigate the problem. You think it's tough getting a repairman in the city — wait until you tell them you live 800 kms away — they suddenly develop an incredibly full workload for the next twelve months and change their phone number just in case you try to ring them again.

Some people, I just found out, refer to Murphy's Law as Sod's Law, which is fairly appropriate I think. Murphy should sod off to where he came from and upset someone else for a change.

Adjusting My Thermostat

Christmas arrived early at our house. After years of subtle hints (crying, sulking, dummy spits and tantrums) I've got an air conditioner in my kitchen. When we first turned it on I was more excited than a kid opening her parcels on Christmas morning.

I've told my family endless times that my thermostat is totally out of whack for living in this country, with summers hot enough to cook your egg on the pavement and winter temperatures that would make the bits on a brass monkey turn blue.

When everyone else is starting to complain it's cold I'm shedding my jumper; when they reckon it's getting warm, I don't know what I'm doing because I've passed out from heat exhaustion. Visiting Tasmania in winter was my idea of fun; everyone else thought I was completely nuts. What they don't realise is that in climates like that winter means putting your feet up by the fire with a good book and a cup of hot Milo — well for tourists and visitors it does anyway. For my friends milking cows at four in the morning it might be a different story.

The only downside to having an air conditioner in the kitchen is that in order to enjoy it I actually have to spend time in there, which doesn't leave much of an excuse for not doing the dishes or the cooking, jobs I've avoided for years with the perfectly reasonable excuse that it was too hot to be in the kitchen.

In the few days since I've had it installed I've actually cleaned my stove, shovelled the dirt and junk off the top of the fridge (the junk is already back and the dirt won't be far behind I suspect), cleaned out my kitchen drawers, washed dishes more than once a day and contemplated cleaning out cupboards. Just contemplated, mind. Now it's my husband who looks like he's going to pass out — from shock!

There is one job that I can probably still avoid though, and that's sweeping the floor. The blast from the air conditioner makes that a pretty pointless exercise. As fast as I sweep up the dirt it blows hell, west and crooked and I'm back to square one. I could always use the vacuum cleaner but that seems to be taking things a bit far I think. And of course I could always turn the air conditioner off while I sweep the floor, but I'm sure it isn't good for it to be turned on and off too frequently. Much better to just leave it on and not worry about the floors; the dirt will still be there come winter.

I'm a bit worried the family will think this sudden enthusiasm for doing things in the kitchen will last all year and I'll be happily cooking, cleaning and doing other things domestic 365 days of the year. But, as I tell them, you need to make any adjustments to your lifestyle gradually, so as to avoid concerns and stresses. I think I should put my feet up, get a good book, a cold drink and let my thermostat adjust gradually. It should be just about right by winter!

There's a Monster in my Laundry

There's a monster in my laundry — a big, white, gleaming monster. I get a shock every time I see it. It's my brand new, shiny, super duper automatic washing machine and unlike my previous little one that tucked neatly into the only space available this one takes up half the laundry.

In fact it is so big we had to renovate the laundry to fit it in. The double troughs had to go to make way for a single one and the new laundry monster. I was quite glad I was away from home when the renovations took place after a phone call to my husband went like this:

Me: Did you get the old troughs out?

Hubby: Yep (he's a talkative sod).

Me: Any problems?

Hubby: Nope — other than the wall came out with the trough!

It was at that point I decided I didn't want or need to know any more.

Fortunately by the time I arrived home the wall had been replaced, a gleaming new trough was in and I was

113

in time to see the grand changeover. Out went my little old machine and in came the new giant.

I couldn't believe how deep the washbowl was. My son has visions of finding me head first in the machine with my feet dangling as I try to reach the clothes in the bottom. Of course I had to try it out right away. It was like a bottomless pit. After putting in a load that would have given my old machine a coronary I had hardly covered the bottom of the new machine.

I'll actually be able to wash the blankets instead of having to get them dry cleaned (once in a blue moon), but I won't be mentioning that too loudly — they'll all want their swag rugs washed.

And this machine is so quiet I hardly know it's going. My other machine used to talk to me, in fact it was more like shouting at full volume and it also tended to get lonely. When it was lonely it would come looking for company until it ran out of power cord. Occasionally it didn't stop even then and choked itself. If this one goes walking I'll be getting out of the way fast.

It's a bit of a worry to find I am actually looking forward to doing the washing. Hopefully the novelty will wear off soon. The only complaint I have is that it doesn't hang out the clothes, bring them in, fold them up and iron them. Then I really would be in heaven!

Anyone Home?

The saying, 'It never rains but it pours' isn't usually applicable these days in the Western Australian Midwest region, so my apologies to those of you looking for rain — but when it comes to visitors, it is so true!

After two weeks in glorious Tassie I was suffering severe withdrawal symptoms. No one to chauffeur me around, cook my meals, keep me entertained and treat me like royalty (the state I've always secretly believed I was born to). To come home to face the schoolroom, the cooking, a mountain of washing and an absence of female company was like stepping under a cold shower in winter.

Then friends phoned to say they were heading north and could they call in on Thursday night? Two couples, fully self contained and great company — absolutely! That was something to look forward to, even if it did mean having to actually do some housework.

Then just yesterday a Registered Training Officer for a tertiary institution 'dropped' in. I saw a golden opportunity to convince my son to do some external study so I requested the RTO to call in again the next day on his way back to Geraldton. 'No worries,' he said, so I gave him a cuppa and sent him on his way.

Next, the phone rings and it is the chap who is to install the satellite dish for the new technology School of the Air are switching to. He will be arriving Thursday afternoon and will need to stay overnight. Okay, just add him to Thursday's guest list.

Thursday morning my is daughter hard at work in the schoolroom when the dog starts barking. On investigating I find a strange man about to leave our yard. Lucky for him the dog's bark is worse than his bite. The stranger tells me he's travelling around picking seed and just thought he'd call in. On leaving he comments 'Dry isn't it?' and heads for greener pastures more likely to present him with seeds.

No sooner have we finished morning tea and are ready to return to the schoolroom when the Training Officer turns up, so it's back to the kitchen, put the kettle back on again and make tea.

By lunchtime I'm exhausted, hardly any school work has been done and I still haven't found anything for tea for our visitors, let alone the family. Talk about feast or famine. Someone out there has a wry sense of humour. They arrange for me to have no visitors until I nearly go crazy, and then they arrange for them all to arrive on the same day to ensure I *do* end up crazy!

The Holiday That Isn't

Two weeks in Perth — what bliss! Or so everyone keeps telling me. Somehow I don't feel exactly that way about it. Wonder why? Maybe it has something to do with trying to juggle appointments to doctors, dentists, orthodontists, skin specialists and podiatrists. Oh, forgot to mention the hairdresser. The optician and physio will have to wait until the next 'holiday'.

In between juggling these appointments we juggled cars (two) for service and repairs, all the time trying to work out who had to be where, what for and at what time. We found ourselves jumping in and out of cars, meeting each other on the doorstep as one or the other of us came or went and hoping that somewhere along the way we had organised for one of us to be taking care of our daughter.

As is this wasn't mad enough I was crazy enough to include a round of Christmas shopping into the mix, which involved asking everyone what they wanted — nothing or everything — cursing products with no prices, cursing people who put things in wrong places, cursing staff who couldn't be found and those who wouldn't leave me alone. In fact I spent a lot of time just cursing — under my breath of course, although on occasion perhaps the odd word slipped out. Maybe that is why people kept a safe distance from me.

I decided in the midst of all this I would treat myself to a remedial massage — I wasn't sure what the remedial part meant but I was hoping it might assist the brain as well as the body. It didn't! In fact it didn't assist anything much at all. It left me feeling like I'd been run over by a truck that had come back for a second attempt just for good measure. The masseur said my muscles were very tight and suggested I have another one in a few days. Not sure why she should think I was the sort of person who had such a liking for pain I'd be willing to inflict it on myself twice in one week.

Added to the mix of our 'holiday' was number two son's final year twelve assembly, followed by his valedictory dinner the next night, speech night a couple of days later and a jaunt around Perth for an entire day viewing girls boarding schools for number three child — oh, and did I mention the two day Women's Advisory Board meeting I had to attend?

Back home now, the car is unpacked, the clothes are put away, the shopping dispersed and I'm starting to unwind. It's beginning to feel like a holiday!

Time for a Makeover

Don't you love the way TV lifestyle shows all take place in the city or just a few miles out in the 'country'? How about a 'real' challenge? Let's take them 'Outback'.

I'd be happy to volunteer my place for a makeover, inside and out. The Backyard Blitz and Ground Force team could share the landscaping. Your yard is HOW big? Which part of it do you want landscaped? The entire half hectare!? Now there's a challenge for you, girls and boys.

There might be a few logistical problems obtaining plants, soil and other necessities but hey, this is television — anything is possible. It's only a four or five hour return trip to Meekatharra if they run out of anything, and 800 ks to Geraldton if it can't be found in Meeka.

It might take a bit longer than forty-eight hours too. Perhaps a week would be better. Aristos could come and cook for everyone. In his spare time he could whip up a few extra dishes and pop them in the freezer for me. About six months supply of meals would be good. Of course he would need to work around all those who were busy with the interior of the house. The team from Better Homes and Gardens repairing, replacing and renovating every room of the house, with the help of the Room for Improvement crew.

Of course sponsors would be falling over themselves to offer me new appliances, floor coverings, curtains and furniture. I will be suitably grateful and scream 'I don't believe it!' and cry touchingly at the appropriate moment of the unveiling.

I might give Changing Rooms a miss though. It doesn't really appeal so much to have someone coming in to completely renovate, renew and replace — all for someone else, especially as they might not be happy with my lack of decorating skills and be baying for blood when it's all over.

Naturally this must all come as a big surprise for me. And since Ernie Dingo is an outback lad himself, I don't mind if he comes and entertains the rest of the family while I could take on his role in the Great Outdoors. Okay Ernie, what's the destination this week? Hawaii — yes, I think I could suffer a week there. Might be a good time to showcase packing tips on one of the shows — I'll volunteer my sponsored luggage and clothing for the cause of a good segment.

What Visitors Can Teach You

Recently we had a visit from my German pen pal and her husband. It was an interesting time and while they learned a lot about Australia, I learned a lot too.

Some of the things I learned (in no particular order):

Expecting visitors can get me cleaning the house where nothing else will, especially overseas visitors.

The more you clean the more there is to clean.

Germans have left hand drive cars — I initially wondered why my friend was climbing into the driver's seat of our car when I picked them up at the airport. Once she saw the steering wheel all was well.

It is not impossible to have a full conversation using two languages, much hand signalling and pictures from a book.

There is no German word for plain flour — after much debate and discussion and the assistance of an electronic translator we eventually decided it's the-flour-you-use-to-make-sauces-with.

Our dog has German heritage — why else would he obey commands in German when he ignores the same ones in English?

Our corrugated gravel road would not even be called a road in Germany.

Kangaroos are sweet and it is not possible to take too many photos of them.

(After a trip to a gold mine.) I never want to be an underground miner — how do they go to the loo with all that gear hanging off you? You wouldn't want to be in a hurry.

Even the most independent of teenagers will ring from the other side of the world if they don't hear from Mum and Dad for a while.

My ability to speak German is on a par with my chance of competing in the Olympic Games or becoming Miss Universe.

Emus are as scarce as hen's teeth when you want to show off to overseas visitors, but appear the minute the plane takes off.

Germans don't like eating Aussie flies either.

Germans do enjoy Australian wines though.

I actually *can* manage seven different evening meals without repeating the same one twice and all seven of them were edible.

Visitors who are happy to entertain themselves some of the time are the best kind.

If you are running late the plane will always be on time — known as Murphy's Law, I believe.

Our visitors have been gone for two weeks now and we are missing them. Already the house is back in the state of chaos it was pre-visitors and the dog still won't do a damned thing I say even when I try to instruct it in German.

The Silly Season

'What do you want for Christmas?' my husband asked, as he does every year. I'm not sure it is possible but what I would really like is my sanity back. So far I have managed to send two Christmas cards to my brother and sister-in-law, forgotten to order the pork for Christmas lunch, haven't even contemplated getting out the tree, let alone decorating it, and am frantically trying to remember where I've hidden the presents. The latter isn't really a problem as I can send the kids on a mission to find them, and you can be sure they will be successful. In fact they probably know where they are right now.

This year (and every other year) I promised myself I was going to be organised. I would make my own cards and they would all be sent out in plenty of time, the presents would be bought and wrapped, likewise the food — well bought, not wrapped. There would be no last minute rush or chaos. Hmm, well, you know the saying, 'The best-laid plans of mice and men go oft awry.' Well it's not just mice and men, let me tell you. Mind you, mice and men are probably the two least likely creatures to get involved in the madness of Christmas.

Despite two trips to Perth in two months the cards still aren't posted, some presents are yet to be chosen, let along bought and wrapped. On the plus side though I have bought a Christmas cake and at the back of the cupboard is a Christmas pudding, purchased on special a few months ago. In fact there are two puddings in the cupboard — maybe I can cross another present off the list!

The tree is tomorrow's project and I'm hoping the kids will be happy to take on that job — without killing each other in the process or wrecking the tree. Of course it will be a completely different story after Christmas when I'm looking for someone to help take all the decorations down and put the tree away.

Once the tree is up and decorated there will be lots of sneaking around with presents. For some reason my family all like to get them under the tree without anyone else seeing what they are up to, which is a bit pointless given the minute a new present is spied under the tree someone will be having a stickybeak at it. Occasionally wrapping paper will give way when the investigation is a little too thorough and then there are howls of protest from the giver. Of course I am far too mature and sensible to be involved in any of those shenanigans, although that one someone has stuck right at the back looks like it might need moving to another spot. And you can't help getting a feel of a parcel when you move it can you?

Amidst all the madness and frantic activity I just have to admit it. I'm just a big kid when it comes to Christmas. Now what did Santa leave in my stocking?

Just Gotta Love Christmas

Why do we set ourselves up every year for a Christmas nightmare? Every year I promise myself *this* Christmas will be a stress free time, then around November something in me snaps. Christmas Craziness kicks in and everyone else ducks for cover so as a) not to get roped into anything they don't want to do and b) to avoid the raging tempest that emanates from their mother/spouse every five minutes in the weeks leading up to the Festive Season.

After years of home schooling my children, I've decided that Christmas follows pretty much the same formula children are instructed to use when writing stories. A story must tell who, why, when, where and what. Christmas is along the same lines.

First comes the *who* — as in who to invite this year? Will it be the in-laws or out-laws? Uncles or aunts, cousins or siblings, friends or enemies? We fall for that trap of thinking we can get on with people at Christmas that we can't stand the sight or sound of for the rest of the year. Funnily enough it always seems the people you invite out of duty rather than an enthusiasm for their company are the ones most likely to be able to make it.

Then comes the *where* (which is closely tied in to the 'who'). Where will the great festive lunch/dinner take place? Will it be their house or ours, the beach or the restaurant, the zoo or the circus? And come to think of it, you actually get the latter two wherever you start up. Suddenly Christmas on a deserted island starts to look good.

The *when* might seem pretty obvious. But not necessarily so, because Christmas can involve at least any of three days: Christmas Eve, Christmas Day, (which includes three meals or more) and then Boxing Day. (I'm sure Boxing Day got its name from the family punch ups that occurred on this day.) Deciding on the *when* involves arguments about who has the longest distance to travel, who went where last year, and placating the I'm-putting-my-foot-down family member who insists they aren't budging from their comfy chair for anyone or anybody, ever.

The *what* is the real killer. What do we buy Jack, Jill and Aunt Betty? Chocolates that will melt in the mail, clothes that won't fit, books that won't get read, toys that break in five minutes so you get the evil curse from both the niece/nephew and its mother. Damn it all: give them all a scratchie and be prepared to fight for your share if they win.

Finally we have the *why?* and that's the one no one can find an answer for. Why do we put ourselves through this, year in, year out? Headaches, arguments, mad cooking sprees, card giving, gift wrapping, tree decorating — we must be mad!

Either that or (shhh! don't tell anyone) we really, despite everything, just love Christmas!

The Twelve Days of Christmas

There are so many Christmas carols but very few of them relate to our Australian way of life. We are starting to hear a few more Australian carols being released and I thought I'd assist the cause by trying my hand at revamping a traditional one to give it more of an Aussie flavour. Below you will find my rendition of the Twelve Days of Christmas in which 'my true love' is a dinky-di Aussie bloke. Hopefully I won't get sued by descendants of the original pen-smith, who presumably departed this life a century or three ago.

This could become a new Aussie Christmas game. Give all the family a pen and some paper and get them to write their Aussie version of a traditional carol. You could have a go at the Twelve Days of Christmas yourself. Maybe you could base it around your mother-in-law and what she might give you. Just remember, if the kids are around keep it clean and no violence please.

So here is the Twelve Days of Christmas — from a sheila's point of view.

On the first day of Christmas my true love gave to me
one sip from his stubby.

On the second day of Christmas my true love gave to me
two meat pies.

On the third day of Christmas my true love gave to me
three odd thongs (the rubber kind, for your feet).

On the fourth day of Christmas my true love gave to me
four dirty shirts to wash.

On the fifth day of Christmas my true love gave to me
five minutes with the remote.

On the sixth day of Christmas my true love gave to me
six burnt snags off the barbie.

On the seventh day of Christmas my true love gave to me
seven fish to gut and cook.

On the eighth day of Christmas my true love gave to me
eight minutes to get lunch and head for the
shearing shed.

On the ninth day of Christmas my true love gave to me
nine swings with his golf club.

On the tenth day of Christmas my true love gave to me
ten minutes notice his mother was coming.

On the eleventh day of Christmas my true love gave to me
eleven pairs of dirty socks to wash.

On the twelfth day of Christmas my true love gave to me
twelve clocks to set to daylight saving time.

Should it become a number one selling hit then I'd just
request a small slice of the royalties — say 75 percent? I
wouldn't like to be too greedy!